GIVIN' THE DEVIL HIS DUE

GIBRAN TARIQ

ROOTS

Gentrification. For quite a long time, I have had mixed emotions about this urban phenomenon of dressing the hood up; the governmental equivalent of playing fairy god-mother. Sure, once the hard-hat heroes with their bulldozers and cranes are long gone and the dust has settled, certainly the neighborhood will look much better, but rarely, if ever, are the original residents allowed to move back in.

What happens, oftentimes, in these cases is that lives are destroyed. When you are forcibly uprooted and displaced, it makes no difference if you were in Bosnia or in Charlotte, the psychic costs are tremendous. They can be life-altering as well.

This morning, I drove through a neighborhood where I had once lived. It was the old Cherry community, the oldest continuous black neighborhood in the city of Charlotte. Rumor and legend have it that the neighborhood was built by the rich, white folks in Myers Park as a housing alternative for the blacks that ran their households.

In any event, the three major hospitals in Charlotte sprung up from the shadows of Cherry with many other medical-related offices and businesses located on the fringes of the community. The fight to steal Cherry went on for decades and the residents of Cherry fought hard to maintain their beloved neighborhood, but how even a fight is it when you are poor and black, and your opponents have the resources of the city at their disposal.

In the late 90s when I lived there, everyone knew that the writing was on the wall and that "the white folks were going to take Cherry." Everyone knew, and no one liked it. Even the hustlers on the block thought it was foul what was happening to Cherry.

What I loved about Cherry was that no one ever left——until now. If you were born in Cherry, then chances are good that you would die in Cherry. That's just how close-knit the community was. So, yes, I was visibly disturbed by what I saw as I drove through the empty streets. I mean, there is no doubting the intrinsic beauty and appeal of the "new" Cherry, but it has no soul. Without a doubt, Cherry is gone. I virtually traversed every single street in the neighborhood, recounting numerous heart-warming memories, and I will be the first to admit that despite the gentrification of Cherry, what I saw this morning was a travesty, a mockery of all that had once been there. I mean, I had to park, and take some deep breaths, to simply digest the enormity of what was actually happening. I was mortified.

Upon my arrival home, I immediately called friends who had lived in Cherry, and their sentiments echoed mine. They felt cheated. And I understood much too clearly.

1964!

I had been twelve. I had come home from being outside playing with my beloved cat, Puff, and I spied a group of neighborhood folk in the kitchen. They were talking quietly in hushed voices I had never heard used before, but I knew what it was. It was the muffled aura of fear. I was shooed back out in the hot, summer sun to ponder what the implications of that gathering would be, and my initial impression was that it would not be good. It wasn't.

We had to move. The white people had decided to raze First Ward to the ground and to build a sparkling, new housing projects in its place. No one wanted to leave, and many tears were shed. This was a watershed moment for me because First Ward was not just a place—First Ward was my life. My cousins and aunts stayed directly across the streets. I had siblings around the corner. I had siblings down the street. I had family and friends everywhere.

All of a sudden, I was asked to abandon the one spot on earth where I felt I belonged. In this blessed place, my earliest memories had been forged. My first kiss was here, my first fight, my first bicycle ride, my first sex. This was the best place on earth, a desolate outpost where the sounds of James Brown blared from almost every open window, and where the smell of fried chicken and collard greens hung over the neighborhood like an aromatic cloud of southern-fried warmth. Where was I to go?!

Needless to say, we were dispersed throughout the city like rolling cactus across a wind-blown desert. Our family went one way, and my other siblings went in another direction, while my other siblings went even further away. I felt fragmented, somehow bent, but by no means broken. What I had to suffer most was that I would be the first one in my family not to attend Second Ward High School. To attend Second Ward was a badge of honor, and it would be unthinkable for anyone who lived, and who breathed the air of First Ward, to dare dream of going anywhere else other than Second Ward.

Back in the days, high school was as good as it got educationally for people in First Ward, so Second Ward represented the zenith of one's academic career. Second Ward was the ghetto version of Harvard or Yale, and I could hardly await my time to go there. When we moved on the corner of Sixth and Davidson Street, I would stand in my backyard, and stare transfixed at the high-schoolers as they marched past en-route to school. They were like a black army of pig-tailed, booby-soxed girls flanked by sun-kissed boys with waves in their hair so thick you could get seasick from looking. I was fascinated, and day after day, I watched this majestic parade, knowing that one day I would join this caravan of blackness knowing, for certain, that I would walk right beside my dearly beloved cousin, Marian, who had taught me to write.

Okay, I got over it, a'ight, but my grades plummeted. I lost complete interest in school and I roamed the hallways of Piedmont Junior High like some dark menace. I jumped on my Science teacher, pulled a knife on my Arts teacher, and when I had taken all that I could take, I stormed into the Principal's office, and demanded my book fees back since the books weren't teaching me shit. I came to school only when I felt like it, and for the peace this gave the teachers, I was awarded a social promotion to the 8th grade.

Apparently, the 8th grade teachers didn't wish to be bothered with me either, so I was farmed out to an all-boys' school in Winston-Salem, called The Advancement School, for the remainder of the school year. It was then, in 1966, that I got the first inkling that the rage building inside me would either purify me or crucify me. To date, it has done both.

It had been no secret in my neighborhood that I was destined for future greatness because all my life I had heard the proud whispers of the elders about just how far I would ultimately go in life. I was the peewee messiah of Sixth Street, the prized kid of First Ward who was going to wow the world and I, for certain, had been equipped with all the mental skills required to claw my way to the top. By the time I was ten, I was a whiz at Scrabble, had a library fit for a king, and possessed a large desk and typewriter. I had mastered the dictionary, had worn numerous awards for my poetry, and just as soon as I had taught myself to type, I, quite naturally, completed my first novel.

Shit happens. After being displaced, I spiritually imploded, and the change was immediately catastrophic. Within a year, I was in Reform School for assaulting a police officer. I served one year and a day, and a few months later on the day that Dr. MLK was assassinated, I was sentenced to four years in prison where I was the youngest convict there. I was still a juvenile, only 15. Upon my release at 19, I went to NY to join the Black Panthers, but got hooked on heroin instead, and embarked on a bank robbery spree that ended in an early morning shootout in the streets of Charlotte. After adding more time to my prison term by a daring prison break, I was released after ten years inside. 90 days after my release, I was framed by CMPD for a crime I did not commit, but nevertheless spent another ten years locked up for the robbery. A few years after my release, I was captured and arrested by the DEA and the FBI as the alleged kingpin of a notorious heroin distribution ring. Oops, there went another ten years of my life.

My troubles commenced the very same moment, I WAS DISPLACED! At sixty-six years old, I am the official poster-child for DISPLACEMENT, and I testify, with every fiber of my being, that I steadfastly believe that the root cause of all my woes are a direct result of the inherent trauma associated with the consequences of social displacement.

Let this be a lesson to anyone who will listen: DISPLACEMENT is a dispossession that destroyed my soul.

FIGHT GENTRIFICATION AND DISPLACEMENT!

END ENVIRONMENTAL RACISM!

Author's Note:

"The pic on the cover dates back to the 1950s and is a photo of the author standing in his beloved First Ward prior to being uprooted and displaced."

CHAPTER ONE

It was saw-dust dry, but sometimes it was like that when the rain had been spare in September. It was bad news, but it gave men something to talk about. Or to complain about. However, Victor Seams was not given much to either talking or complaining. He just wanted to get a full day's work out of his construction crew. He didn't drive them though since they all knew what he expected of them.

"Kenny," he yelled, "swing that crane about forty-five degrees more that-a-way and pull up that stump. It's got to go, so might as well get it up now."

The crane operator mumbled a dirty remark as he fiddled with the gears, forcing the outstretched neck of the crane high into the air, and then making it swoop down like a great, yellow bird, digging into the ground.

"Dammit, Kenny, pay attention," Victor snapped. "You missed by a mile."

After another attempt, Kenny snickered. "How's that?"

Victor started to curse, but his good eye spotted something shining in the bucket of the crane. He squinted in the sunshine as he waited for Kenny to dump the dirt beside the uprooted stump, and when he did, a shiny box tumbled out.

Kenny spotted it as well. He jumped from the seat of the crane, seemingly drawn by the iridescent sparkle of the metal box. "What do you think that is?" he questioned Victor, trying to conceal his excitement.

"Don't much know," Victor explained, "but it sure the hell ain't Blackbeard's gold because ain't nobody lived in this housing project but dirt, poor niggers. This is Earle Village, remember, a very unlikely place to find a box of gold."

"Maybe, not that, but how about some bank robbery money? You said yourself that that this was s high crime area years ago." Kenny licked his lips in anticipation. "You never know," he reverently croaked, "just could be our lucky day. Could be a drug-dealer buried that box and it's all filled up with twenty dollar bills."

"Or hundred dollar bills."

They slowly approached the pile of dirt where the box glistened, but suddenly started pushing and shoving each other as they clawed and grappled with one another, attempting to seize the box first; to claim it for himself.

Kenny dove headlong into the mound of debris, reaching; arms outstretched.

Victor pulled his legs, yanking, tugging him back.

Kenny, his mouth filled with dirt, swung.

Victor ducked the punch.

Both men squared off, facing each other, ready to fight.

"Wait," Victor sighed, his shoulders sagging. "We split."

"Fifty-fifty?"

"Yeah, it's only right, I guess"

They sealed the deal with a handshake, and then Victor reached into the pile and retrieved the box. It was heavy. Reluctantly, he handed it to Kenny. "You can open it."

Kenny was emotionally touched. "Why, by golly, thanks, Vic. I apologize for taking a swing at you a second ago. Kinda lost my head."

"That's over with. Now, open the box."

The box was gun-metal grey with a pair of separate clasps. Kenny popped them both, and in a solemn act of contrition, held the unlocked box out, awarding Victor the honor of flipping the lid.

"What in tarnation!" Victor angrily yelped. "A dead cat."

Kenny peeked over the top of the lid, and then dropped the box in disgust. "Oh shit, man," he cursed. "A stinking, dead-assed cat." He angrily kicked up a storm of dirt into the open cat casket. "What dumb nigger would bury a stupid, fucking cat in a strong box?"

HIs dream of instant wealth spoiled, Victor turned business-like. "Alright, the party is over. Let's get back to work."

"Damn," Kenny wailed, "it's dry as shit."

From behind them, the whole mound of dirt and debris seemed to move, and a terrible sound emanated from back there. Even as they turned, the noise got louder, closer. It was a howling, an agonizing, wounded noise.

"What the hell?" Victor exclaimed in disbelief.

"But-but that cat is---was---dead," Kenny declared. "How ca----?"

The cat tore into him, leaping at his face, plucking his eyes from his head.

"Get him off me! Get him off me!" Kenny screamed, but before Victor could think of what to do, the cat slashed a razor-like claw across Kenny's throat, severing his jugular. Bright, red blood spurted from the gash. Then Victor was next.

The tiny cat's teeth sank viciously into Victor's skull while his hind legs, with their razor-sharp talons, raked his face, forcing their way through the thick layer of skin into the interior of his brain. He plopped to the ground, and very slowly died. Kenny, who lie beside him, was already a corpse.

The cat looked up from the killing field into the serene, blue sky, raising up on her hind legs, sniffing the air. A gentle breeze blew in from the northeast, and the tabby screwed up her delicate nose, wrinkling it as she caught the scent of some delightful smell far, far to the west.

Suddenly, the feline became a happy creature. She darted off, racing with swift, quiet steps, bounding towards uptown. She stopped often, sniffing with great animation, ferreting out the one scent that made her delirious.

Darkness was a pregnant blackness in Dalton Village, and at around 7:30, Roscoe Brown thought he heard scratching outside his door. He ignored it, but the scratching came again. The sound became even louder. Now, it was a thumping, and Roscoe sat up straight. This time, there was no mistaking it.

Something was right outside his front door, but then he heard another sound that froze his blood, that altered his heartbeat. It came once more,

"*Meow!*"

What chiefly struck Roscoe was fear, the full-grown sense of hell about to break loose, yet he dutifully trudged to the door, and opened it slightly.

"Welcome back, Puff," he groaned.

The yellow cat leaped joyfully into Roscoe Brown's arms, happily licking the man's callused hands.

"I guess you'll be wanting some milk. It's a long way from Earle Village." He carted Puff into the kitchen on his shoulder. "Long time, no see," he uttered as he removed a saucer from the shelf. He stepped to the refrigerator, and got the milk out. "Everything is low-fat now, Puff," he explained, pouring, "except mice, but," he stared at the cat, "they were never your thing, nohow." He reached down, patting the cat lovingly, his eyes filling with tears. "Dammit, white folks," he shouted hoarsely, "just can't leave well enough alone, can you? Didn't y'all learn anything the last time?"

He looked at Puff, lapping milk. "Evidently not," he gasped.

The old black man reckoned that Charlotte would soon be topsy-turvy, tipsy with terror in the days ahead. Puff would see to that. Hell had just been unleashed, and at fifty years of age, he was too old to stop the carnage. He would simply retire to a dark corner in his soul to mourn and to pray. The city would need it because it was about to be exposed to a scourge from which there would be no protection.

Roscoe Brown admitted to himself that he didn't know much, but he knew his cat, Puff, so he knew better than anyone else what was about to happen. He also knew why. He recalled vividly.

When he was a little boy, he had lived in First Ward. He had been born on a Monday that rained, and for the next twelve years had lived in the exact, same place where he had been born, a brown, three-roomed, shotgun shack sandwiched between poverty and pain on Sixth Street where the paper-thin houses appeared to grow out of the concrete like colorful matchbooks. Yet, First Ward had been a nigger Garden of Eden. There were grocery stores. Alexander's on Sixth and Caldwell. Wright's on Fifth and Davidson; Tutterow's on Seventh, and farther up the block was Funderburke's. There were not as many churches a stores, but First Ward had a pair of grand ones: Little Rock AME Zion where his family attended, and there was Mount Sanai where the black Baptists worshipped. Even had a school, and of course, a funeral home. Everyone, Methodists and Baptists, went there.

However, the place that had fascinated ROscoe most as a boy had been the one place he, and all the other children, were forbidden to go---the creek! Nothing would grow there and it stank terribly.

Everyone stayed away from the creek, but not Roscoe. He liked this forbidden part of the neighborhood. He didn't like the stench, or the ugliness, but he adored the aloneness. No one was ever there, so despite the fact that the quaint, little haven burned with an unquenchable, invisible fire that smelled like sulfur and tar, he got used to it. Never mind that it was rocky and flat, oozing with pockets of bubbling sludge, he liked it still.

Some of the old folks thought he was strange; a lonely boy, always alone, always sad. His family gave him a kitten and Roscoe instantly fell in love with the tiny, furry creature. Roscoe named the cat, Puff, and they ate, played, and did everything together so for a time, Roscoe was happy.

And then, one day, Puff died mysteriously.

The sudden death of the cat penetrated Roscoe's soul, and for two long days, he grappled with his private grief, but at the urging of the old folks, he laid the cat to rest. It had been on a dark, black night when God had commanded the thunder to be noisy and loud, and had instructed the blades of lightning to be white-hot and sharp, that he had committed Puff to the earth. The heavy sheets of rain had burst down upon him with almighty rush, but he would not hurry his footsteps.

He had marched slowly.

Faces with sad eyes had peeked out of dirt stained windows as family and friends had watched him trudge silently by. Everyone knew where he was going and no one dared to stop him. Roscoe neared the creek, and there next to a tree stump that bordered the filthy, fetid water, he had dug a small grave. What he had said, no one had ever asked, and it very well may have been that he didn't say anything at all, but what everyone clearly recalled though had been the painful, blood-curdling scream. Roscoe had thrown back his head and the terrible sound had flown from his soul. It had rent the whole block, and then Roscoe had shoved mud into the hole and ran home. No one had ever seen him run before.

And now Puff was back from the dead. AGAIN! The first time had been in 1964 when the neighborhood had been destroyed to make way for Earle Village, a low-income housing projects. All had gone well until.......

Shouldn't they had known?

All had gone well until they had disturbed Puff's grave, and now that have done went and done it again.

Oh shit!

Seth Jacobs didn't look away. He was an old man now. He stared vacantly.

The bodies, tarnished by death, rested upon the cold slab, gruesome in the ugly caliber of horrid mortification, yet starkly wholesome in the timeless manner of eternal repose. Even at its most cruelest, death imposed a tranquil calm.

No active sentiments pronounced themselves to Jacobs. Neither were there any bitter thoughts, so he simply nodded. "Yep," he said library quiet after a while, "I have seen this before." He spun around on his heels, leaving. "And once was enough." He stopped at the morgue's door. "I don't know what perception you may have of me, so I'll explain." He pointed at the mangled bodies. "When it comes to that, I'm the most sensible man in the world which means I want you to leave me alone."

"B-but you were there," Police Chief Heywood Smalls said. "You are our only link between now and then."

Jacobs chuckled mirthlessly. "In 1964, I had to be there. I was the chief investigator so I couldn't duck, dodge or run for cover. Now, I can."

"But whatever it was is back. What does that do to you?"

Makes me want to stay alive, mainly, and that's a sensible reaction for someone who has experienced the hell that is about to revisit this city." Jacobs pushed on the door. "Ain't going to pretty."

Heywood Smalls followed the old man into the hallway. "Do you believe this city deserves the kind of holocaust you know is coming?"

"Hmmph," Jacobs snorted, "I still don't believe they deserved it the first time."

"Then you must help."

Jacobs walked faster, trying to get away. "You'd be a damn fool to count on me as the defender of this city's impending doom. Shit like that does not excite me any longer."

Catching up, Smalls gripped the older man's thin shoulders. He pleaded. "Help us."

"This is an encore," Jacobs lectured. "Then, as now, the carnage began in Earle Village, only then it wasn't Earle Village yet. It was still First Ward, but they were razing the neighborhood to make way for what was to become Earle Village. Anyway, the first people killed then, like now, were construction workers on the job site, and from what you have indicated, it seemed like almost in the same exact spot."

"What is it about that spot?"

Jacobs shrugged. "Your guess is as good as mine."

"A burial ground, perhaps?"

"Good guess, but no. First Ward, at the time, was a rundown slum. No graveyards. No haunted houses. No headless horsemen. Sorry."

"But it had to be something."

"I agree," Jacobs snapped, "I'm just telling you what it wasn't." Calming down, he spoke softly. "The moon was of a pale sheen that night in '64 when I finally got my first peek at the bodies. They were shredded viciously, their hearts ripped from their chests. Men stood around the scene in varying degrees of unmistakable fright. We all wanted to run away and to hide. That moon," he whispered mournfully. "I'll never forget that moon, usually so noble and assuring, but that night, it was not itself. It was if the moon, that night, had been coerced into providing such a haunting spotlight for unspeakable horror, and that was proof enough for me to know that we were dealing with something otherworldly, supernatural."

"Why, Charlotte, though?"

"How the hell I know," Jacobs cracked. "All I know is that it is back."

"Oh God!" Smalls groaned.

"Only thing different, though, is that the killings are heading in a different direction. Same pattern, though, but in '64, the trail of bodies led to Piedmont Courts. This time, they point towards West Boulevard, that area. Breathe in the darkness between the links of the chain," Jacobs rasped darkly. "First Ward......Piedmont Courts.........West Boulevard. It's there that you will find an answer. Whether or not, it will be enough to save you from that demonic force, who knows." He grimaced. "Just remember," he added, "to leave me alone."

CHAPTER TWO

When he saw the sign welcoming them to Charlotte, Clinton McCall turned to his family and smiled. "I hope they have tennis courts here."

"They've got sunshine," his wife, Meg declared, "so they have tennis courts."

"Guess who is from Charlotte?" Brittany, the fifteen year old, red-haired daughter, quizzed.

"Who?" Everyone, including eight year old Aaron wanted to know. "Who?" he chimed. "Who?"

"Jodeci," Brittany proudly responded, "that's who. They're my favorite singing group."

"Now, listen," Clinton said. "This moving to a new place will be new to all of us so we will have to pitch in to make it work. Whenever a problem arises with anyone, it is a family matter, okay. Remember that, please, Brittany and Aaron. No one shuts anyone else out. Am I coming through loud and clear?"

Clinton McCall was a lean, fit, dark-haired forty years old, Seahawks fan and had spent all his life in Seattle. So had Meg, his red-haired wife, who at thirty eight had longed for a more sunny climate. The topic of relocation had come up at various times during their happy marriage, but it was just talk, nothing more. However, when an opening for a branch manager had come open in Charlotte, Meg had urged her husband to go for it. What could it hurt, she had prompted.

Clinton McCall got the job.

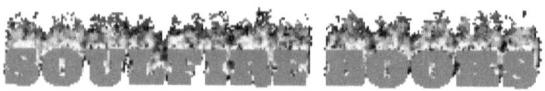

One week later.

At the official ribbon-cutting ceremony, even though there was no scientific reason for it, there appeared to be a hysterical, emotional destructive anxiety that settled over First Ward like a collapsing rooftop, and without prelude or preamble, everyone somehow related to it.

One lady voiced concern. "For some reason, all of a sudden, I want to go back home."

An elderly man spoke to the man at his elbow. "If you ask me, it feels like we are being welcomed to hell." He tried to make it sound funny.

"Well, at least, the homes are lovely," one lady remarked. "Doesn't appear to be the kind that would be haunted."

"Hell," her husband snorted, "as expensive as they are, maybe they should come with ghosts to help out around the house. I just hope they do windows." He glared at his wife. "You sure as hell don't."

Clinton McCall merely sat in the hard, folding chair, hunting for an explanation for why he felt so tense. He hummed a few bars of his favorite song as a distraction, but the feeling still lingered, not going away. He stared lovingly at his wife and children. They seemed cheerful enough so maybe it was just him. Maybe this was stress from the new experience of packing up ad moving to a new, strange city.

Moments later, everyone commenced clapping when the newly-elected Mayor approached the podium with a few local dignitaries in tow. They all beamed with accomplishment.

"Doesn't this day just bristle with energy," Mayor Paul Matthews gushed happily, "and why shouldn't it? This is a major breakthrough for this city as we open up and dedicate another corridor of this still-developing community. Just a mere decade ago, an undertaking of this nature would have been scoffed at, but today, Charlotte and only a few other select cities across the country are making this great idea a reality. If I'm not mistaken," the Mayor chuckled, "but our city, the Queen City, is perhaps only the third city in the entire nation where this type of neighborhood has been planned, but we intend to make our model work better than anywhere else in the world."

Thunderous applause.

"This will be a truly, wholly integrated community where the stigma of race and income will be total diminished. Living together, side-by-side, white and black, the fortunate right beside the not-so-fortunate. This is a concept whose time is overdue, and I personally urge others to abandon their one-race neighborhood and move here. Let's show the world how it's done, Charlotte."

More applause.

The Mayor continued. "I can think of no better role model for underprivileged kids than to witness the success of others from their own neighborhoods. These children will no longer have to look up to drug-dealers and petty crooks for inspiration because now, right on the streets where they live, they will have the example of bank presidents and civic leaders. Down with thugs and up with hugs," he chanted.

Roscoe didn't clap. Puff didn't purr. They were both simply there, watching the neighborhood being turned over to outsiders and strangers. The pain cut like a knife. This is how it had to feel, Roscoe noted, when China was forced to cede Hong Kong to the British Empire ninety-nine years ago.

After a brief introduction, Roscoe watched without expression as his aunt Dr. Mildred Baxter Davis, addressed the crowd. Roscoe listened to her and was swollen with pride, but wished he had become a musician instead of a janitor. His aunt would have liked that since she was the one who had given him a set of drums when he was about seven years old.

The next speaker was a city councilman, Arthur Davis, but Roscoe knew him as "Crack", fondly recalling the countless times he had stood by as a peewee, watching Crack, Cheetah Hoke, Kenny Johnson, and Harry Fuller play basketball in the Sixth Street alley.

The last speaker was Vilma Leake, a newly-minted school board member who had moved into First Ward when her husband, the late Reverend George Leake had been pastor of Little Rock AME Zion Church on Seventh and Myers Streets.

Roscoe had been baptized at Little Rock when he was a boy, and he knew every nook and cranny of the church as he and George Leake Jr., Sidney Roach, and other young boys had explored every inch of the building, playing when they should have been in Sunday school. That church, now converted to The Afro-American Cultural Center was only one of two buildings that remained intact from First Ward's glory days. The other was the elementary school on Ninth Street.

Puff clawed the air.

Abruptly, the Mayor and the other dignitaries stepped down from the stage, huddling close together for the customary photo shoot where everyone smiled so prettily. Roscoe spotted Sonja Gantt. She was pretty. Roscoe held Puff up so she could see, but the cat wasn't interested. Instead, her attention was fixed on a white, teenaged girl off in the distance. Uh-oh, Roscoe thought. Puff's gonna get that bitch!

With the snipping of the ribbon, loud cheers erupted as another section of First Ward was now up for grabs. Roscoe ambled through the crowd, mumbling to himself.

Puff darted off to where the white girl was, and Roscoe ran to get her. This syrupy fantasy version of First Ward with its tree-lined streets and cozy homes sickened him, sending his spirits into a downward spiral, toppling into a cauldron pit where his anger circulated like hissing vipers. His anger was short-lived. The white girl disarmed him.

"Hello, sir," she offered politely. "That's such a beautiful cat. What's her name?"

"Puff."

"Hello, Puff," the girl said, making a funny face. "Can we be friends?" She shook Puff's paw daintily. "Are you moving here, too?"

"No, I just came out to watch the ceremony." He paused. "I used to live here a long time ago."

The girl was perceptive. "You sounded so sad when you said that. Why?" she asked.

Roscoe was momentarily surprised.

"Oh, yes, by the way, my name is Brittany." She extended her hand.

"And I'm Roscoe John Calvin Frederick Brown. Pleased to meet you."

"Really?"

"Really."

Brittany seemed elated. "No one has ever been pleased to meet me before."

"Well, now that the tradition has started," Roscoe smiled, "I'm just the first among many."

A man rushed up and lightly scolded Brittany. "We had hoped that you hadn't gone far."

"Mother, father," Brittany intoned properly, "I'd like for you to meet my new friend, Mr. Brown."

"Roscoe," he corrected, offering his hand. "And who might this be?"

"That's Aaron, my brother. Guess what, Mr. Brown used to live here a long, long time ago."

"Is that so," Clinton quizzed. "You intending on a second tour of duty in First Ward. I don't know what it was like before, but it sure is beautiful now." He gazed around in wonder. "Just where did you live?"

"Don't ask him that," Brittany wailed. It's makes him sad."

"We're sorry," Meg apologized, "we had no idea."

Roscoe laughed aloud. "I would be pleased to take you on a trip though the yesteryears of First Ward." His eyes twinkled. What strange, friendly white folks. If they knew what was good for them, they would get the hell out of First Ward before it was too late because when it came to Puff, mercy was nonexistent. He might be able to induce Puff to spare the girl, but a whole family. He didn't know about that.

"Houses along this corridor were very modest," Roscoe said. "Simple, wood houses. No one had any money. You see right there," he pointed. "Used to be a grocery store, and behind that was a big, wide field, and behind that on Davidson Street was where my great-grandmother lived, right smack dab in the middle of the block. Probably had the most beautiful house in First Ward."

"Show us. Show us," Brittany begged. "Can we, dad?"

"That's up to Mr., er, Roscoe, honey. I sure could use the exercise."

They walked a half block or so. "Right there. My great-grandmother, Amanda Morris, lived right there, precisely. There was no other house like it in First Ward." Roscoe's voice grew distant, nostalgic. "It was all red-brick, pretty. Even had a two car garage out back and guess what, there were two cars in them. The house was so magnificent that it looked like it belonged somewhere else, some place better. The floors were shiny all the time, and in one room was a beautiful piano with huge chandeliers. It made me feel rich just to be inside that wonderful home. Her oldest daughter, Jessie Mae, was my grandmother, and three of her sisters, Margie, Ruth, and Kat, were English teachers." Roscoe chuckled. "Everyone said that I should have been a writer because of my strong English background. My grandmother introduced me to poetry when I was very, very young and she used to write poetry when she was a girl. I used to---." Roscoe felt embarrassed. He coughed and changed the subject. "And right here," he commented, moving to the corner, "I'll never forget the day I saw two guys fighting. I was the only one around. I was about ten, and the guys were about seventeen or eighteen. I didn't know either of them because they were not from around here, but they fought for what seemed like an hour. They started right here and then they rolled down the hill in what used to be a culvert which was about fifteen feet deep. They stayed down there, fighting and I stayed up here, watching."

"What were they fighting for?"

"I don't know," Roscoe remarked solemnly, "but it had to be important to them because there was no one around to cheer them on, to urge them, no one for them to show out for. I never saw two men fight like that before or since. Hope I never do, either."

They walked back up Davidson Street.

"The first girl that openly admitted she liked me lived right there. Her name was Loretta Smith. I haven't seen her since we moved in 64. Anyway, just above her house, up the street a bit, there was a hill and my friend, Desi, lived on the top of the hill. I hadn't seen him for over thirty years, but he was at my cousin, Cassandra's funeral, and we recognized each other immediately."

"Where was your house?" Aaron wanted to know.

"Two blocks from where we stand." Roscoe spoke softly.

"Can we------?"

"Maybe some other time," Roscoe interjected. He knew that would not be such a good idea because he knew the closer he got to his old home, the harder it would be for him to cope. Plus, Puff was getting moody, so Roscoe took this as a cue to part ways with the strange, white family. "So long," he muttered, hurrying off.

He didn't look to ever see them again.

From a safe distance, he watched the family of four disappear around a corner. Roscoe sighed. He leaned against a lamp post and closed his eyes. In an instant, memories of days gone by flashed in his mind. Roscoe watched happily.

The ceremony of adventure clutched at his chest when, at once, the door to his old house flew open and he and Puff bounced joyfully down the wooden, rickety steps to play in the rugged familiarity of Sixth Street. They ran, boy and cat, past the rotten tree in front of the house that was filled with shiny, colorful lizards.

With synchronized symmetry, they both scampered across the street, stopping briefly in the yard where his cousin, Lil Calvin, lived. He and Calvin were born on the same day, so they would dress up alike and pretend they were twins, but they fooled no one. He was too tall. From there, they darted, as quick as a lizard, across the field and stood underneath the makeshift basketball goal, a bicycle rim nailed to a board. It was here on this dirt court where he had scored his first two points. The shot had not come easy. He had to work for it, using all the skill at his disposal, but with it came the applause and approval of all the other players who were already "on the books." Oh what a fine and magnificent moment that had been: his first two points ever.

A little later on, he bumped into the memory of the time when he had played first base on that blisteringly hot day when Al Ronnie hit three homeruns to help lift Sixth Street over Fifth Street in a heated softball game. He remembered it well. Later, he sat down on an empty crate outside the fence of the Johnson house where every Sunday, Kenny, the middle son, would regale him with colorful narratives of the latest movies he had seen. Tauras Bubber.....The Days of The Trifids.....Hercules Unchained. No one could tell stories like Kenny Johnson. It was almost like you were there. Roscoe smiled, recalling the time Kenny had told him a story so scary that he couldn't sleep for three nights. It was funny now, but it sure was no laughing matter then. In fact, Roscoe's Mama, Louise, told Kenny not to ever tell her son any more ghost storie!

There were so many wonderful memories here. And then there was the creek! It was like standing on the brink of some kind of cataclysmic afterbirth. The stinking, tar-black water seeped down low into a heaped-up vale of mud and slime that poured obscenely into the wide, crooked oval of the creek's mouth. Bald-faced, moss-slick rocks were distributed here and there upon the face of this expressionless hell, and next to the stump, Puff's empty grave; a toxic, barren womb.

And then Roscoe experienced it. Blinding rage. Terrible fury. He was incensed, angered. He felt obliged to redeem his memories, to rescue them from being tarnished, buried like Puff had been, under mounds of dung. He would not permit intruders to trample upon the ancient beauty that was

First Ward because white folks could only, would only desecrate the joy, spit upon the memories as though they were orphans, making a mockery of everything he had once held dear. In the process, Roscoe knew they would bury him as well for once you robbed a man----any man----of his cherished memories, then you have, in effect, assassinated that individual. Roscoe would not be buried. First Ward was sacred ground.

The last image in Roscoe's mind was the summer of 64, the year he was emotionally murdered. Roscoe hated 64. Just as soon as the announcement was made that First Ward was being demolished, another incident instantly came to be, and Roscoe was as frightened as a twelve year old could possibly be.

In 1964, shit got real! Not only did he have to move, but Roscoe and all the other school children would be forced into all-white schools. Integration was being born and the pangs of the birth scarred and scared Roscoe. As the first blacks allowed in white public schools en masse, First Ward was thrown into spiritual turmoil. All the grown folks from one end of First Ward to the other were terrified at the prospect of how we, their children, were going to be destroyed by learning just how dumb we were. They figured it would be no way for us to compete with white students especially when we studied from their old, cast-away books.

On Sixth Street, all the fun and games of summer ceased as everyone from the preachers to the pimps tried, in whatever way they could, to prepare us for what awaited us academically. On Sundays, the sermons were not about Jesus. The whole text revolved around how we were representatives of the whole colored race and that we had to do good. We had to prove ourselves. Roscoe felt like he carried the weight of the world on his puny shoulders, and it only got worse when his beloved Grandmother,

Jessie Mae, pulled him aside and told him that she was counting on him not to fail.

And just like that, Roscoe grew up. Angry and mad.

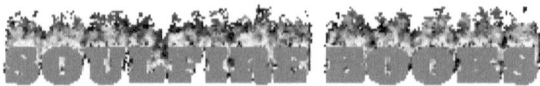

Night-time eased into First Ward like a distinguished charlatan, bringing not so much the darkness, but a cover for the practice of evil. In houses up and down Eighth Street, domestic tranquility was in retreat, and the unsuspecting families had no idea what was happening to them. They were angry.

"Bitch!" the well-heeled CEO screamed at his socialite wife. "I told you not to be fucking with my music. Now, put Too Short back on before I have to kick off in your fat ass."

"You, white trash motherfucker," the wife responded in her crisp, British accent, "you put one finger on me and you going to jail."

Meanwhile…across the street.

The pregnant woman arose from the plush sectional sofa. "Honey," she explained to her husband, "I've got a strange craving for something different."

"What? Ice cream with a pickle." The husband chuckled, knowing that pregnant women often developed odd taste when in the family way.

"No,"

"Popcorn and hot sauce?"

"Not that either."

"A peanut butter and French fry sandwich."

"No."

Bob was stumped. He was clueless.

"You know what I really want, honey?"

"What?"

"Some crack. And get me a stem also. I think that what they call the little pipes they smoke with."

One block over.....

"Henry, all our credit cards are charged to their limits."

"It's okay, dear. Don't worry about a thing."

"Are you going to take out a second mortgage on the summer house?"

"Nope."

"Then what are you going to do, rob your own bank?"

"Yes."

"How marvelous," the wife gushed. "May I help?"

And on it went throughout the neighborhood until by the time dawn had arrived, there had been fourteen 911 calls for assistance. Roscoe was pleased. From the high-rise hotel room he had rented for the night, he was well-acquainted with the mayhem going on below. From his window, he could peek right into First Ward and each time he looked, he would see either the flashing lights of a police car or a fire truck either entering or leaving the neighborhood.

"Damn," one of the paramedics confided to a cop. "It wasn't this bad when the darkies lived here. You'd think that right-minded, decent white folks would know how to act, but hell, they're carrying on like a bunch of niggers."

These were Roscoe's exact sentiments. The incoming white people were cursed, tainted with the spirit of the black family who had lived in the spot where their pretty townhouses now stood. Roscoe laughed. "And this is just the beginning." He laughed some more, tickling Puff. He recalled the Hawkins family from off his block on Sixth Street. Oh shit, the white family that invaded that space were going to be hard to handle. They would be a special kind of crazy. Roscoe howled with glee.

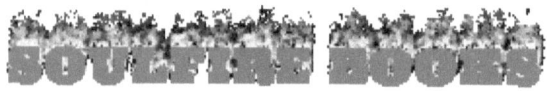

In the light of day, the night jitters of First Ward were treated as harmless boo-boos and swept under the rug. No one wanted the Mayor to hear of them. What? And tarnish his image of First Ward as Utopia. For the time being, the 911 calls never happened, the fighting was nothing more than dirty dancing, and all the spilled blood was ketchup. Still, Police Chief Heywood Smalls, a strapping six-foot, blond male with droopy eyes and an even droopier mustache, was concerned as hell.

Smalls' primary concern right now was trying to figure out just what had made the people of First Ward go bananas like that. What had spooked them? It was as though the newcomers were acting like the wild bunch that had lived there before them. That thought amused Smalls, but he wasn't laughing. What if First Ward, in a spiritually convoluted way, was a haunted badlands, and no matter who you put there, they were going to shoot and cut each other up. Maybe, First

Ward had a mystique that branded you with evil. Now, Smalls laughed. He could not imagine a posse of Ivy-League white teens in Duckhead shirts ad Dockers, running around smoking blunts and brandishing automatic weapons.

Nothing made sense.

CHAPTER THREE

When Roscoe had attended Alexander Street Elementary School, it was all-black, and Piedmont Courts was all-white with only a narrow twenty-five feet wide creek and a three foot chain-link fence separating the two. At recess, kids on both sides of the creek would approach to get a good look at each other. This, more than likely, was the first time either had experienced children of the other race, but once the novelty and the giggles of the experience wore thin, vicious rock battles began. This was war. White kids on one side of the creek and black kids on the other, throwing rocks like they were hand grenades. This went on day after day throughout the entire school year. Their parents had never thought to discourage them, and our teachers had never sought to restrain us. Guess they felt it was on-the-job training for the coming race war.

Roscoe smiled at the memory. Piedmont Courts had been a good place to live until the night Puff had showed up. 1964, It had been unseasonably, unreasonably cold, and nature had cursed the earth with bitter, biting winds that had howled in from the northeast with such wintry bluster that everything was hardened with icy frost. The early evening seem to decay like a rotting tooth, fermenting an abscess of menace.

And then came Puff.

Roscoe, at midnight, had been snatched from the remote world of a wet dream and slapped into a rude awakening. His body seemed to weep as sweat oozed from every pore, the humid stench of fear circling the room like combustible energy waiting to burst into open flames. He felt consumed with anxiety, and a dark voice, sinister and authoritative, emanating from everywhere, made him get up and go answer the door.

Roscoe had trudged through the quiet house, his family peacefully asleep, his feet slipping noiselessly over the cold, concrete floor. Fear rushed from all their hiding places inside his skull, and he felt senseless, powerless to halt his advance through the apartment so he continued through the hallway, down the stairs, and to the kitchen door. Here, he was allowed to pause, but outside, he could hear the swooping down of the angry wind as it rustled through the dead leaves, shaking them up and hurling them against apartment 358.

At the door, his hands had lost their heaviness and one of them, he didn't remember which one, had reached out and had turned the knob. Half surprised that a ghost or a goblin had not awaited him outside, Roscoe had suddenly glanced down and there at his bare, black ankles was Puff. She caressed his legs and then sashayed into the kitchen.

At once, Roscoe had been terribly horrified for he knew this was no illusion. This was real. This was Puff and she was back from the dead.

Roscoe had fainted.

Morning had found Roscoe tucked comfortably under the bedcovers, snoozing gently, but as soon as his eyes had opened, he flung off the final crust of sleep and peeked around him. At his feet was Puff. She rose, purring and playful, the innocent blood of numerous men still damp upon her paws. And then he understood everything. Puff was back because God had answered his prayer. Now, it made sense.

That day had been bright and sunny, jubilant. It was May 1964. Roscoe had burst into the house with Puff in tow, laughing happily. Then he received the news. The white folks had decided that their neighborhood was not fit to live in, and that they were going to destroy it.

"But why, Mama?" Roscoe had asked.

"The white folks can do as they please, so we have got to go."

"Where will we go, Mama?"

"I don't know yet, but we'll find somewhere."

"But will my uncles and aunts and cousins be coming too? What about Ves and them?"

"They'll be going somewhere, boy, but probably not where we going, though."

"But I love it here, Mama. I don't want to move nowhere else. Suppose I don't never get to see Marian ever again?"

"We've got to move," Roscoe's Mother had tearfully said, "and that's all that's to it."

"But, Mama, where will Marian go?"

"Boy, we don't even know where we are going yet. Plus, Marian won't stop being your cousin because you might not see her no more."

Roscoe had burst out of the house, almost hysterical. He cried sadly. If they made him move, he told Puff, the white man was going to be sorry.

Under the house, he had hugged his beloved cat to his chest, sobbing uncontrollably. He vividly recalled what he told his cat on that fateful day in '64.

"Puff," Roscoe had moaned, "if they tear our neighborhood down and take Marian away from me, then when you die, I pray that you come back as a saber-toothed tiger and kill 'em all."

Later that same day, Puff mysteriously died.

Roscoe had buried him two days later. The 12th of May.

And now, five months later, Puff was back.

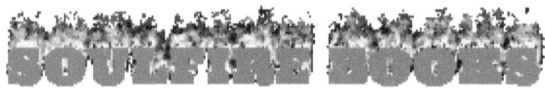

Puff entered the open door. The girl was asleep, and the soft glow of the moon fell diagonally across her face like a pale, yellow ceremonial mask. Her scent, pleasant and penetrating, easily overpowered the faint aroma of greasy, junk food that hung lightly in the air.

The cat sprung onto the bed, not disturbing the girl's sleep. She neared closer to the face of the girl and pressed her cold nose to the girl's cheek. The girl was sweet and enticing; alluring.

Slight noise down the hallway aroused Puff to attention and she jumped quickly to the floor and out into a larger room to the left where the approaching footsteps grew closer.

Clinton McCall hurriedly dashed to his daughter's room and swiftly turned ON the light. Brittany didn't move. Hearing her relaxed breathing, his own breathing returned to normal, but before he turned the light OFF, he searched through her closet and then peeked under her bed. Satisfied, he plunged the room back into darkness and went back to lie beside his wife.

Without delay, sleep rushed in upon him from all sides, but just as he descended close to the welcoming sensation of a full-fledged dream, he felt partly roused by a nagging curiosity that there was an invader in his home. He also sensed that the intruder had come to ravish his daughter. Quitting the throes of sleep, McCall regained complete consciousness greeted by the oppressive rattle and hum of dormant fear. He raced again to this daughter's room, his feet beating heavily upon the plush carpet. He, once more, saw that the girl was safe, but the fear would not go away so he sought a place against the wall by the doorway and slid down into a sitting position.

He would stake-out here.

Movement, what little there was of it, seemed to reverberate from the game room next door. He advanced at a slow pace------creeping. The vast room was overhung with darkness, but the light stayed OFF as he swept the room with his eyes, twin brawlers out to detect anything amiss. As soon as he had absorbed all the information the darkness would allow him, he flooded the room with light. *But all was well.*

Mickey Mouse. Barney. Elmo. They were all accounted for. Other toys littered the room in neat, little clusters giving the impression that nothing had been disturbed. The closet door was ajar, though. He peeped in. Piles and piles of stuffed, furry animals. McCall noticed how real the playthings looked, the stuffed yellow cat more so than any of the others.

He went back to his daughter's bedroom.

The threatening menace of only a moment ago was gone. It had vanished. McCall held his tired head between his hands, trying to shake the severity of what he had experienced. It had been like coils of hellfire had been laid upon his chest, and he confessed to himself that it had been overwhelmingly frightening. He placed a wet kiss upon his daughter's forehead and marched back down to the master bedroom. His wife awaited him, sitting in the middle of the bed.

"Did you see anything?" she asked.

"Huh?"

"You felt what I felt, so you went to check on Brittany. Was she okay?"

"You-you sensed that-that too?" McCall stammered. "You-you felt that Brittany was in danger?"

"Very clearly."

For the rest of the night, Brittany slept with her parents while outside Puff walked through the shadows, and as a consequence, the denizens of First Ward gnashed their teeth for surely they felt that hellhounds were nipping at their heels.

As the yellow car drew near to any home, the terrible enormity of approaching death would grow swollen, giving way to such fierce misery that an elderly man expired, his heart refusing to beat.

Puff came closer.

And closer.

Turned away.

Came back. Closer still.

The excruciating, demonic veneer of fright was so excessive it wrung the oxygen from the air until Clinton McCall and his wife were literally suffocating, gulping in air as heavy as stones. Thick curtains of immense blackness drew them into a void where each found themselves slipping away from each other, tumbling toward the abyss.

Brittany screamed.

The darkness dissipated.

And then they thought of Aaron.

When the family reached his room, the door was closed and McCall grappled with the knob. It wasn't locked. Frantic, he rushed into the room and found that his son's face was blue, impassive with the expressionless mask of death setting in. Aaron's chest was still.

"Call 911!" McCall barked. *"Tell them it's an emergency."*

McCall performed CPR on his son and within seconds, the boy's chest expanded, filling with air, heaving up and down on its own. Meg cried in relief. McCall felt like they had cheated death as the beautiful crescent of pink slowly returned to Aaron's cheeks. Instantly, Brittany felt blessed.

He was divorced. His kids were grown. He was a thirty year law enforcement veteran. He enjoyed listening to the blues. But was he ready to die? All of these thoughts consumed Smalls as he drove from Piedmont Courts across town to West Boulevard. He turned into

Dalton Village, smugly assuring himself that this housing project was the third and final point in the triad.

He hitched this notion to the fact that the trail of bodies led them to West Boulevard. There the trail died, but Dalton Village was the nearest housing project and the thing---whatever it was---seemed to possess an affinity for such places.

Another thing that sparked his interest in Dalton Village as being door number three was the recent fact that just last week, 24.5 million dollars had been allocated to raze the projects and remake it over in the image of First Ward with tree-lined streets and luxury apartments. Redevelopment, it seemed, was a connection because this creature, for whatever reason, was violently opposed to urban revitalization.

Yet.

Maybe the info he now had was the last thing he actually needed because more unresolved questions about "yellow cat" was totally like wiping your nose with the back of your hand and then not having any place to wipe the oozing, slimy snot that glistens on your fingers. Yellow Cat was like that.

The McCall boy, Aaron, was close to being a tomato because of something very terrifying he had seen, but when asked what it had been, all he would mutter was Yellow Cat. It just didn't figure. How could anyone equate a yellow cat with unspeakable terror?

When he had examined the McCall's home, he could detect no visible signs of forced entry and nothing in the house had been disturbed, but the Mama, Papa, and the red-haired daughter all confessed to experiencing a presence in their home last night. Sadly, none of them could explain what it was and this upset Smalls because it didn't provide him with anything on which to turn left or right. He was simply stuck in the middle-------with Yellow Cat.

And then there was the Murphy throat slashing on Myers Street. Was Yellow Cat responsible for that also. Smalls wanted answer quickly. He needed a clean place to wipe the snot from his hand.

He exited the Interstate and cruised into Cherry where he parked on the far end of Waco Street and knocked like the police.

"Come on in this house and let me get a good look at you to see if it's really you or not." Grandma was a big, black, jovial woman who, in her younger days, could fight and drink just as good as any man in either of the Carolinas. At seventy, she was still growing strong.

After a few minutes of chit-chat, Smalls popped the question foremost in his mind. "Who is Yellow Cat?"

"Never heard tell of no Yellow Cat, did know of a pretty, yellow gal named Cat, but she upped and died of a drug overdose way back about twenty-five years ago. The only other Cat I knew was Top Cat. As many times as you busted him, I know you ain't forgot his ass. Oh yeah, there was Cat-Cat, the drag queen. She dead now, been 'bout ten years. Sang like Aretha. Grandma shrugged her beefy shoulders. "That help?"

"Not much," Small admitted, "but I figured that if anyone knew about Yellow Cat, it would be you. More people came through the doors of your liquor hose than came through the church doors."

"Well, honey, sometimes folks need something a lil more stronger than the gospel."

"But no Yellow Cat?"

"Believe me, I knew 'em all." She shook her head. "No Yellow Cat. I was there when they changed the diapers on First Ward both times and I'm telling you straight from my heart that ain't no hustler, ho, square, Christian, or everyday nigger never came through named Yellow Cat."

"Then maybe Yellow Cat is some kind of presence."

"You mean a h'ant or a spook?" Grandma's eyes got big, growing white. "Boy, don't you go messing 'round in the spirit world. If Yellow Cat is a ghost, your best bet is to leave it be."

Smalls sighed. "Wish I could walk away from this one, but I can't."

"This lil white boy you was telling me about that got messed up in the head. Where he live?"

"On Eighth Street."

"By my old juke joint?"

"Two doors up, I reckon."

Growing quiet, Grandma calculated, thinking back. "That would be about where ol' Abraham and his wife, Sarah, stayed. Yeah, that would be just about right," she said, drawing her words out slowly. "Sho'ly would. Um-hmm. That.....you know, they had a young'un, bout eight years old when it-------." She stopped talking, her words freezing.

'When what?!" Smalls shrieked desperately. "Come on, Grandma," he pleaded helplessly, "talk to me." He grabbed the big woman's hands. "What do you remember?"

Grandma went limp. "Goodness gracious," she moaned. "Feel like my head 'bout to split in two."

"It's okay, Granma. It's okay. Nothing is going to happen to you. I promise you that, but you have to tell me about that boy. What was it, Grandma?"

"The young'un's name was Isaac and when he was just about eight years old, the same age as that white young'un, he went into shock.....he got his head all messed up just like that white boy. Isaac saw the white man who ran the store shoot his uncle and kill him. Then they all said that Isaac was a vegetable, just like what you said they said about that other young'un, the white one."

Smalls didn't know what to think.

"And that ain't the half of it," Grandma remarked slowly. "If that white man who got his throat cut lived on Myers Street where I think he did, then there's something else you gotta know." She hesitated. "Did that Murphy man live in the area just behind Little Rock Church?"

Smalls nodded.

Grandma looked scared. "Something bad done gone wrong, Heywood, because that's where James Luther used to live. He-he got is throat cut."

Smalls still didn't know what to think.

Oh sweet Jesus," Grandma wailed. "The white folks be dying just like niggers did." She shook her head over and over again. "The chickens done come home to roost."

At last, Smalls understood.

CHAPTER FOUR

The day they buried Paul Murphy, it almost rained. The oily-looking sky was fenced in by a pit of massive, gravel-grey clouds that sulked across the evening horizon, heaped up like dirty pillow cases.

Clinton McCall offered a silent prayer for the dead and tried to submerge himself into the celebration at the bank. He stood for a brief moment at the fringes of the hoopla, measuring how odd he felt. The gaiety and frolic were seemingly obscene gestures to him in view of his son's hospitalization. The contrived merriment disturbed him, but yet he smiled and saluted, toasting the bank's latest acquisition.

It had just been confirmed this morning that First Union would pay 17.5 billion dollars to acquire CoreShares Financial Corporation in Philadelphia, making this the most expensive banking deal in US history.

McCall executed a dismally bland whoop as he slapped Jack lambert on the shoulder as he excused himself to his office. He wished to call his wife, Dialing the number, he peered out of the window. The sky still struggled furiously to churn out rain as flashes of jagged lightning skimmed the heavens, painting white-hot smiles on the dirty faces of the clouds. Just then a car entered the parking lot. McCall smiled. It was Roscoe whom he had hired to clean up the bank. McCall made himself a mental note to make sure that Roscoe got a big slice of the cake.

"Hello, sweetheart," McCall spoke into the receiver. "I should be leaving here in a few more minutes. Roscoe just drove up to clean the bank, so that is as good an excuse as any to cap off the party."

"Tell Roscoe I said hi."

"Will do. He's getting his supplies out of the car now------*what the hell!?*"

"Honey, what's wrong?"

"Oh, it's nothing, really. It's just that I have never seen a cat move that fast before. It was like a yellow blur. Meg," McCall choked, "Roscoe's cat is yellow."

"Yes, I know, but Puff is just a harmless tabby."

"I'm not so sure of that anymore," McCall responded sharply ."You didn't see what I just saw. I mean, well, uh, it was amazing, but that kind of speed for a cat, even a cheetah. Puff was on those birds before they knew it, and if she had wanted one, he would been dinner. It was weird."

"Clint, look, I hate to burst your bubble, but I'm afraid I must. It was an illusion."

McCall was incredulous. "You're telling me that what I saw perfectly was an illusion."

"Yes, and we both must be careful or else our minds will take us on a wild goose chase, playing all sorts of tricks with our minds." Meg paused. "At the onset of a tragedy such as ours, it really is quite normal."

"I see, and just where did you learn all this?"

"Miss Putnam, at the hospital."

"Trust me, Meg, I know what I saw, and I'm reporting this to Chief Smalls."

"Honey, please don't. I've even mentioned Puff to Miss Putnam, and in her professional opinion, feels that since Aaron was so enamored of Puff, and since he couldn't or didn't own the cat, he had a bad dream where he may have imputed bad qualities to Puff in a subconscious effort to stifle his desire to possess her."

"Do you really believe that, sweetheart?"

"Listen to me, Clint," Meg pouted, "the premise is not as far-fetched as you would make it out to be. Remember when we were dating in high school? What did I tell you each and every time I got mad at you. I would tell you that I hated you, and though it was the biggest lie I could tell, it made it easier for me to stay mad at you. It works much better for kids."

"Well, I suppose," McCall conceded.

"That's my boy," Meg cooed. "Everything is going to be just fine. Trust me."

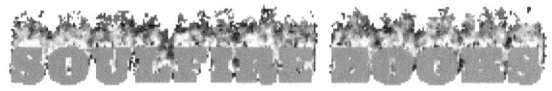

Smalls was drinking more regularly now, and everyone seemed to have a ready comment about how tired or how thin he looked. Most times, he would respond light-heartedly or would mockingly exclaim that he was a fit as a fiddle.

But if only they knew.

This case was threatening to ruin his sanity, and he knew he had to talk to someone soon. Occasionally, his gaze periodically studied the short list of names he had prepared. At the top of the list was James Ferguson II, a prominent, black attorney. Beneath him on the list was William Bluford, a professor at JCSU, who was thought to be the most intellectual black person in the country. Other names on the list included Reverend Brenda Tapia, Reverend James Barnett, General Gregory, and Dr. James Samuels whose church, Little Rock, sat in the heart of First Ward.

Smalls pondered the list, about to choose when he recalled someone else: Charlie. He grinned widely. Charlie Jones. He congratulated himself with another drink. Why hadn't he thought of Charlie before now? Anyway, Charlie had been an usher at the old Savoy Theater in the old Brooklyn neighborhood. If anyone could help, it would be Charlie because as Charlie himself was fond of saying: "The one thing I knows about is niggers."

A minute later.

"Charlie!?"

"Whoever you might be, you know good and damn well it's Charlie. Who else gonna be answering my damn phone."

It was Charlie all right. "Look, this is Heywood Smalls."

"You got a warrant," Charlie joked.

"I need to talk to you, my friend. Bad."

"Bring me a drink and get on over here." Charlie laughed. "The cheaper the juice, the less I talk. You still remember how it go. Cheap juice-----."

"Don't make lips loose."

Forty-five minutes later.

"Yeah," Charlie agreed, "that's quite a ballgame you got going on there and I figures you're about right about the creature being kinda stuck on First Ward. I mean, like you said, the only two times it has caused problems was when they go to tearing that old neighborhood down. And yeah, I do remember the killings in 64."

"But what do you think about the land being cursed? Maybe something happened there long ago. Hell, you said yourself that black people are superstitious and believed in voo-doo strongly when you were a kid. One thing I do know is that whenever that piece of land is disturbed, all hell breaks loose." Smalls sat on the edge of his chair. "Do you know anybody who that ever sold their soul to the devil?"

"Shit, Heywood. Any nigger, in the old days, who got ahead, or had anything worth anything was accused of being in cahoots with the devil and I don't doubt it. As hard as white folks were on us back then, a nigger needed all the help he could get. The way it was then, wasn't too much difference in the white man having your body and the devil having your soul. Either way, a black man had a long row to hoe."

Smalls sighed. "Suppose Charlotte had a crossroads, you know, the place where those blues singers and musicians went to meet the devil if they wanted to exchange their souls for earthly fame and fortune. They say that was why blues legend Robert Johnson was so great." Smalls shrugged. "Who's to say, that there as not a crossroad in Charlotte?"

"And it was in First Ward?"

"Yep, and so that spot is fixed with a mojo; a spiritual do-not-disturb sign. You buy that?"

Charlie frowned. "I wouldn't bet my boots on it."

"Okay, then," Smalls winked. "Give me the history on First Ward."

Charlie grew reflective. "In around 1860, Charlotte had 17,000 people, seven thousand were slaves, and the slaves were kept in the rural areas until after the civil war when they started to move to the city. Around this time, the cheapest places to stay, if you were black, was in Second Ward mainly because it was built over creeks. That is where I was born, right there in Brooklyn. Blue Heaven was also on that side of town. Anyway, round 'bout that same time, I imagine blacks began moving into First Ward although I can't say for sure." He looked at Smalls. "You remember the late Charles Kuralt, the white man who used to be on TV. Well, I heard that he lived in First Ward on Ninth Street which means that white people occupied the neighborhood before they moved out. I don't know when they left"

"Probably just as soon as the blacks started moving in."

"More than likely, that's a fact. Anyway, by 1890, this whole city was totally segregated and this forced the opening of the very first black public school which was Myers Street Elementary School. Was located in Second Ward. The next year, Charlotte got its first and only black hospital, Good Samaritan." Charlie winced. "If black folks in this city ever had reason to cling to a clump of land as sacred, it would be where Good Sam once stood. That hospital was a Godsend, saved countless, black lives. If you were black, I don't care how much money or prestige you had, you didn't get into one of those white hospitals. Good Sam was all we had." Charlie laughed sadly. "Guess what site is in the same, exact spot where that wonderful hospital was?"

"What?"

"Ericsson Stadium, home of the Carolina Panthers." Charlie shook his head in mock disbelief. "People getting hurt in the same spot where they used to get healed. Ain't that something? Anyway, throughout the first two decades of the 1900s, Second Ward was very prosperous, our very own black Wall Street. Second Ward was a stunning success, proving what blacks could and would do if given the chance."

Smalls threw his hands up in resignation. "Sorry."

"It be like that sometimes," Charlie commented wearily. "Anyway, First Ward, while not as prosperous as Second Ward, was considered a good place to lay your hat, but about forty years later, the people at HUD, the housing and development folks, got too big for their britches and decided to do black folks a solid by tearing down their homes and forcing then to seek shelter elsewhere. I remember it like it was yesterday. Those, excuse the expression, crackers came riding in on their bulldozers and cranes like they were the goddamn cavalry, scattering black folks to the wind every which way. Urban Renewal, the prize of integration, broke niggers up like pretzels."

"But if those neighborhoods were so prosperous, why did they fail?"

"Neglect and abandonment by the city, mainly, but more than anything else, it was racism and spite. In 1904, blacks weren't allowed to use the public library so to justify this, the city authorized the construction of a brand new library for blacks."

"Did they build it?"

"Yeah, they built it, a'ight," Charlie spat. "It was just an empty building without a single book and nary a stick of furniture. Some library, huh? Man, no neighborhood can remain strong when the city turns its back on it, neglecting to provide something as basic as hot water, but there's more." He opened a drawer and removed a photo album. He flipped to a yellowed newspaper article. It was from The Charlotte Observer. The date was September 22nd, 1912. "Read that."

Smalls read aloud. *"The Second Ward is populated by blacks, many owning comfortable homes, but farsighted men believe that eventually this section must sooner or later be utilized by the white population."*

Charlie had heard enough. "The white folks weren't going to let us be, nohow, but that was a dirty trick. They knew all the damn time, they was going to take Second Ward away from us just as soon as we made it into a black paradise. That was some bullshit, man. Second Ward was nothing but a swamp, infested with snakes and mosquitoes. It was unfit for human habitation, but yet we went in there. We drained the swamps, we killed the snakes, we built a neighborhood from scratch. Countless black lives were lost in this valiant, colossal struggle to turn an unforgiving swamp into a thriving black metropolis, and we did it. We did, Heywood, and we had every right to be proud, but them white folks were watching, just waiting for the right moment to take it all back. Bastards!" Charlie needed a drink. "As quiet as it's kept, urban renewal was simply an eviction notice. The same thing happened in First Ward, they just got to Second Ward first." Charlie took a sip. "I don't know about the crossroads shit you talking, but maybe the thing you talking 'bout might not be nothing but the buried souls of black folks in First Ward coming back to haunt white folks."

"Why not Second Ward, especially since it had more to be mad about than First Ward."

"Because when we got evicted from Second Ward, we remained pretty intact. We migrated as a community to the Westside, so our bonds of kinship weren't shattered or damaged. First Ward was not so lucky. That community, which had been together for decades, was split up and sent every which-a-way. Not only were relatives separated, but also members of the same household. Some of the larger families who couldn't accommodate themselves in the smaller houses that were offered them were forced to divide the family in half with some living in one place; the other half, miles away." Charlie snorted in rage. Second Ward got evicted. First Ward got displaced, so yeah, maybe it's like I said. Maybe that thing ain't nothing but the rage of a thousand black souls coming back to make white folks pay for what they done done."

Heywood Smalls was ready to go.

49

That night.

When Smalls entered First Ward, the complexion of the night was a savage dark blue. He silently cross-crossed through the barren shadows, not disturbing or disrupting the texture of their crippling gloom, but welcoming the chance to get away from the turbulent darkness. Lumbering across the street, the moon dashed a pinch of glow onto his face, making it appear slightly more rounded, more full. He moved on. A bit farther, he detected a subtle shift in the atmosphere, one that stank of death and blood.

He had anticipated another killing in First Ward so he dismissed the brooding reluctance inside his head and went into the house. A compact bundle of nervous energy zapped him as he stepped deeper into the living room. The house was quiet, but even in the dark, the house felt sunny.

Smalls climbed the stairs. He counted, not wanting to.

One----Two-----Three.

By now his gun was in his hand, gripped knuckle-aching tight as the hypnotic meter of his breathing had swollen to a fierce snarl. He raised the weapon in readiness as he continued his ascent.

Four-----Five.

The top of the staircase was a blue-carpeted promontory with bedrooms to the east and west. Which way? Which one?

Smalls barely noticed his own hesitation as he quickly moved to his left. That was the room, he decided. The victim would be inside. His heart galloped at full speed as he touched the bedroom's door with his toe. It swung open an inch or two before the thick carpet snagged it, braking all motion, but through the small crack, he could plainly see a body in the bed. What he didn't see was the head.

Smalls walked away from the crime scene. His officers knew what to do. Keep a lid on it and lie like hell.

Smalls felt that he now sat on the verge of breaking ground in this case, and if this call proved fruitful, he felt he would have a bonafide invitation to crack the case. He phoned Charlie.

"Hello, Mr. Know-It-All," Smalls teased. "Do you know anything about the area on Stonewall and Mint Street when you were young?"

"Sho' do. Right up from Second Ward."

"What used to be there on that corner?" Smalls grew tense, hopeful as he awaited an answer. He thought of Hahn Villard's severed head.

Charlie thought, was silent. Then spoke. "That was where the train station used to be. Yeah, sho' was. Southern Railway."

Smalls breathed deeply. "Listen closely, now. Was there a black man from First Ward that you know of that ever get his head cut off and left in front of the station?"

"How you know 'bout that? Was before your time?"

Smalls was excited. "But did it happen?"

"Yeah, it happened. The man was Alonzo. White man kilt him and stuck his head on a pole in front of the station 'cause they wanted a wall to separate the black and white waiting areas. I guess he figured that the only way to draw attention to his problem was to murder an innocent man."

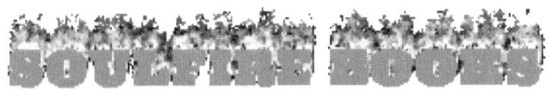

October blew past, taking Halloween with it, and Smalls uttered a prayer of thanksgiving. He had been sure that something bitterly horrible would occur in First Ward as a senseless pagan tribute to halloween, but night had passed uninterrupted by violence or mayhem. Maybe it was over? He foolishly prayed that Halloween had been the coda, the end theme of this madness, He hoped that it was now water under the bridge.

Half surprised at his own stupidity, he laughed at himself, shaking so hard that big drops of free roasted coffee spilled out of his cup on top of the mass of paperwork on the kitchen table. He wiped furiously. He had spent the last week, amassing death certificates, obituaries, hospital reports, police records, and virtually anything else he could uncover about traumatic deaths in First Ward and Earle Village, dating back to who knows when. He had also made the purchase of a pair of books: "THE BLACK EXPERIENCE IN CHARLOTTE-MECKLENBURG 1850-1920" and, "COLORED CHARLOTTE."

On various occasions, he would admit that he was overwhelmed. There was simply too much info to digest and not enough leisure time to sit around at his table, drinking coffee if it was morning, liquor if it was night, reading about the many ways blacks in First Ward had gotten killed off.

From what he been able to decipher, if whites were dying the same death of earlier deceased blacks from First Ward, then he was certain the trend would mimic only the cases that had shocked the public conscience. For once, he was partially sure he was on the right track.

Anyway, what he learned was that in Charlotte, black and white, in many places lived side-by-side. That is until 1875. Reconstruction. During this period, the legal separation of the races commenced and although the south still favored a cheap source of labor, it didn't want to have to see them after work. Blacks were then herded into their own run-down communities where they were hemmed in by a newly-established white theory of racial superiority. All of a sudden, keeping blacks in their place became all the rage, and Charlotte wasn't about to be a Johnny-Come-Lately.

Circa 1969, a black middle-class emerged in Charlotte and then spearheaded a movement out of the inner-city into the more affluent, outlying white neighborhoods.

Smalls stopped reading to rest his eyes, then started looking over a fresh batch of documents. Some bold print caught his attention. He focused on it.

"Naw.", he chided himself, "too trivial." He pushed the article away, leaned back, and thought about it some more. "Naw," he muttered again. To begin with, the death was too colorless, didn't have the mesmerizing brutality to command one's attention, and was much too trim on the shock. "Naw," he repeated for the third time.

After taking a shit, Smalls was back at the kitchen table. He was busy scribbling notes on a memo pad, writing like crazy. Thanksgiving was next month, and according to the murder he wanted to ignore, but couldn't, the Grim Reaper would be making a house call in First Ward. Again.

Smalls paced. The kitchen seemed to be growing smaller and smaller until there was not a thing left for him to do to sit back down. He would have to break this case on Thanksgiving. He had no other choice. With his head in his hands, the read the article once more.

By nine that night, the temperature had dropped dangerously low, the howling wind livid with a bitter chill that cut to the bone. Three parked police cars sat directly in front of the Perry home on Alexander Street. Another pair of police cars were parked in the rear.

"Nothing in. Nothing out." Smalls' voice crackled on the walkie-talkie. "For all practical purposes that building is sealed. Nobody and I mean nobody gets close. Is that clear?"

All the cars responded in the affirmative. Understood.

"You have explicit permission," Smalls continued, "to employ deadly force at the approach of anyone who does not immediately obey your order to halt. Understood?"

Once more. Affirmative.

Not far away, the man and the cat were about one hundred yards distant, watching. The man, slightly annoyed, stomped his heavily booted foot into the decaying brown grass. Roscoe would have to go back. The cops had the entire perimeter of the apartment enclosed, making human entry impossible so Puff would have to go it alone. No doubt, she knew what to do.

"Go!"

Puff sauntered off into the stiff night breeze, the wind ruffling the short hair of her sleek, elongated body. She sniffed the air, moving swiftly now, her paws only barely touching the ground as she zig-zagged across the empty playground, emerging into the dark shadows on the other side of the street. She slowed now, stopping periodically to stand on her hind legs to softly inhale the frigid vapors of the night, smelling the fear.

Closer she came.

The odor of fear drained out of the men, lining their open pores with the stench of it, marking the invisible night air. Puff swam along in this intoxicating pool, the oily aroma slamming her ears back, deliciously tickling her nose.

Closer.

Officer Shannon couldn't get warm. He was still shaking even though he had the patrol car's heat turned all the way up. "I haven't felt like this since I was in "Nam," he told his partner. "It's almost like my insides are sending me a memo, telling me to get the hell out before it gets too late."

"I-I know what you mean," his partner groaned. "Something's coming down and it is going to be bad. Even now, I feel like our heads are in the lion's mouth."

"I don't get it."

"What's to get, man. Something is out there and it's getting closer." He pulled out his weapon. "Shoot anything that moves."

A fine, misty rain added even more gloom to the night as the cat, hidden by a clump of dead shrubs, stretched. She meowed gently, the sound a low-pitched rumble.

"Y-you hear that?"

"Yeah, you bet I did. But what was it?"

"I don't know," Officer Shannon answered. "Better see how the others are doing."

Officer Ernest Jackson washed down the corrosive fear with a gospel song. He sang loudly, hoping his voice would seep into the evil and soothe it, turning it OFF.

Not far off, Puff scampered out of her hiding place about forty feet from the three police cars parked end-to-end in front of the apartment, and the area immediately erupted into open anxiety, igniting fires of sheer panic in the officers.

"Oh my God," Shannon groaned pitifully. Help!"

The rain began to pour down, and mighty sheets of freeze-dried ice splattered down upon the earth, beating mud puddles into the ground. Then, Puff scurried past and the enormous fear abated.

"Damn," Hoolihan gasped, "what was that all about?"

"We better be more concerned about if it's over than about what it was."

The partners nodded at each other glumly.

"Damn cat is going to get soaked if she doesn't get out of the rain." Still a bit edgy, Shannon rasped. "You didn't see nobody, did you?"

"Nope. Just like the Chief said. Nothing in. Nothing out. We're covered."

The cruel howling of the wind and rain churned violently for a few more minutes, reducing itself to a mournful hum, then whistled to a stop. Now, all that was heard was the greedy, gurgling noise of flowing water being emptied into the sewer, but the temperament of the night never got friendly.

In the darkness, Puff scaled the walls of the apartment, clawing her way up, digging through the bricks, going paw over paw until she was on the roof.

Upstairs, Scott Perry was shaken. He heard noise, the sound hollowing out, deepening. He ran to the phone, dialed 911. "I am not alone." He croaked once more. "I AM NOT ALONE!"

The line went dead.

Perry stared at the receiver vacantly, not understanding at first, then knowing exactly, he uttered a gasp of fright. He fled down the steps, his feet thudding woodenly, clumsily as he bounded to the bottom.

Puff came through the chimney!

Perry ran to the phone in the kitchen. "*911!*" he panted, snatching the receiver up. "*911!*" Finding the line dead, he dropped the phone and darted through the living room just as the entire wall above the fireplace disintegrated; shards of broken brick exploding into the room like a detonated bomb.

"Jesus!" one of the officers outside yelled. "What was that?!"

Instantly, the men burst from their squad cars and crashed through the door of Scott Perry's apartment, and instantly they saw Scott Perry, but instantly knew they were too late.

Smalls was on the prowl again. Each of the officers had spoken with vivid clarity. No human had breached their security boundary, and all the reports had been the same. *No* one *had breached their security perimeter!*

"Tell me more, Officer Shannon. Just what did you see?"

"I didn't see anything, sir. Not a thing."

"What did you hear, then? What did you feel?"

"I heard an explosion. That is when we went in."

"And?"

"The whole interior living room wall had been demolished as if it had been dynamited."

"Was thee anything visible or noticeable to indicate a bomb or any sort of explosive device, Officer Shannon?"

"That is negative, sir. There was nothing to establish that an incendiary device had been used."

"Than what do you personally think destroyed that wall. Please don't hesitate to guess."

"Sir, I have no idea, but whatever it was, it couldn't have been human because whatever it was, it came down the chimney and popped through the wall like it was toilet paper."

"Before then, what?"

Officer Shannon sighed. "I-I was afraid, sir."

"Of what?"

"Of nothing mortal or human. There was a presence there, sir, if you're willing to believe that."

"I'm not here to judge," Smalls intoned. "I'm just looking for answers. When you say presence, what do you mean exactly?"

"All of a sudden," Shannon said remembering, "I got cold. Colder than I have ever been in my life and I couldn't get warm, and then in the same way that I had gotten cold, I got scared. Then, it starting raining real hard." Shannon paused. "I just know that nothing of this world and I swear that nothing human crossed our barrier."

"Nothing?"

Shannon sighed tiredly. "Well, a cat, but nothing else."

"*A cat?!*" Smalls fought to hold his voice steady. "J-just what color was the cat, Officer Shannon, if you recall?" His voice trembled slightly. "Do you recall the color of the cat?"

"Yellow, sir. The cat was yellow."

CHAPTER FIVE

The lady though he was a crackpot.

"You want what?" she asked again.

"Access to any files you may have concerning treatment or surgery of all yellow cats in this city dating back to 1964."

"Are you serious?"

Smalls nodded.

Miss Lawson glared at the uniform. "What did the cat do?" she snickered, "get shot in a bank robbery or maybe it's that you have your Dr. Seuss' mixed up. Could it be that you're looking for the Grinch? He's the one that stole Christmas. The cat was in the hat, remember?"

Smalls was not amused. "May I speak to someone else?"

"Gladly." She pressed an intercom button. She spoke. "There is a police officer here to ask you a few questions about the Cheshire cat."

"Cheshire cat?!" the animal doctor inquired.

"I'm sending him right in." She faced Smalls. "Two doors down, then left."

The middle-aged man stood from behind the desk as Smalls entered the office. He extended his hand. "My name is Ferdinand Macklin, head veterinarian. How may I help you?"

"I'm searching for info on a yellow cat."

"Any yellow cat in particular?'

"Yes, but there is a problem."

"Which is?"

"I don't know how to distinguish him----or her--- from the countless other yellow cats in Mecklenburg County."

"Excuse me," the vet exclaimed, stifling laughter, "but now I recognize the reason for Miss Lawson's apparent humor."

"Ah her," Smalls acknowledged, a real Rosie O'Donnell type. Anyway, can you help me?"

The vet rubbed his chin thoughtfully. "I do have a suggestion. Why don't you just turn McGruff, the crime dog, loose on him? After all, who would possibly be better chasing a cat than a dog?"

"You find this humorous, don't you?"

"Very much so."

"Well, it's serious. Very much so." Smalls leaned towards the vet. "And I want help."

Macklin leaned across the desk, towards Smalls. "Look, Chief,I have no idea why you came here, but I---we—can't help." He jumped up and dashed to a long, tan filing cabinet, and began pulling the compartment doors open. "Come," he invited, "there are no yellow cats here."

"Were you here in 64?'

"1964? No, and neither was this clinic. In 1964, let me see. I was in elementary school. A candy bar was a dime, cigarettes, slightly more, and the only bad cops were in the movies. My, how times have changed."

Smalls got out of his seat, walked over to the file cabinets, closing each of the drawers gently. "Since no yellow cats are hiding in there, what about technical information?"

"Such as?"

"Mind if I sit back down?"

Macklin sighed warily. "What do you want now?"

"There are steroids for animals, am I correct?"

"Yes, there are steroids for animals."

"Is it possible that an animal, say a cat, came in here wounded and was pumped full of steroids, could this induce, uh, bizarre behavior. Could it make the feline abnormally strong?"

"Comparatively speaking, what measure do we employ to determine what is abnormally strong for a cat. What would that be to you? The capacity to beat up two Rottweilers." He shrugged noncommittally. "The ability to freefall off the roof of The Radisson and not get hurt? See how difficult that is because first you must come to terms with what is meant by abnormally strong, and at any rate, cats or any pets, for that matter, are not injected with steroids for quite the same reason that a football player or a pro wrestler would inject himself. We, veterinarians, prescribe or introduce steroids as a treatment and not as a glorified means to super-strength, so I doubt very seriously if you will encounter a souped-up Supercat while out on patrol."

Smalls started to speak.

The vet composed himself briefly. "It is not possible" MacklIn interceded quickly, "but don't take my word for it. Go," he admonished, "get a second opinion. Ask questions elsewhere. There is The Charlotte Cat Clinic over on Kings Drive. Excellent place. Have you ever met Doctor Bissell. She knows a whole lot more about cats than I do, and if she is not authority enough, there is The Emergency Veterinary Clinic on Elizabeth Avenue, and guess what, both are only a stone's throw from the police department headquarters."

Smalls remained seated. "Do you know of any other means by which an animal can be transformed from ordinary to supernatural?"

"Yes, I do, Chief Smalls, "and it's called Hollywood. MGM can do it quicker than you can eat a doughnut." Macklin pushed his glasses up on his nose. "I'm sorry I couldn't be of more assistance, but if you insist on getting a court order, go right ahead."

"Have a nice day," Smalls said.

Heading back to his vehicle, Smalls felt almost vindicated because, at last, he had what he thought was sufficient proof to believe that Yellow Cat was just that---a yellow cat, but how in the hell was he capable of the things that had been done in his name. That was especially frightening now because it was so hard to explain. The fact that yellow cat was not a man stopped Smalls dead in his tracks since a killer cat bore no similarity to any serial killers, past or present. No case had ever entered his life like this.

By definition, Smalls still didn't believe that now since he had an idea what he was chasing, there was still no guarantee he would or could bring it to justice. Starting now, he didn't know what was real and the sooner he made peace with that fact, the better. As far as he could see, the creature lived or belonged to someone in First Ward pre 1964, and that the animal had died or was buried in that spot where the creek used to be. All that made sense. A pet cat in a shallow grave. He had no problem with that whatever, but what did perplex him was trying to piece together what came next.

How did a dead cat come back to life? Why?

A hush fell over Smalls' mind as someone banged on the door. "Come in, Mr. McCall, Glad you could make it."

"You sounded urgent."

"And for good cause. Have a seat." Smalls smiled at his visitor. "If you don't mind, I'd like to get right down to business." Smalls drummed his fingers on the desk before speaking. "I now have every reason to believe that your son really did see a yellow cat on the night he went into trauma."

"Yes," McCall admitted, "I know."

"*You know?!*"

"What, about the yellow cat?"

"Yes, dammit," Smalls blurted angrily, "about the cat. Why in the world would you withhold this valuable piece of information?"

"It didn't seem relevant."

"My God, McCall, what could you have been thinking? *You didn't feel it was relevant!*" He drummed with his fingers. "How long have you known?"

"First, Chief Smalls, I feel you are blowing this way out of context. Puff is nothing------."

"*Puff?*"

"Yes, the yellow cat. Her name is Puff."

"Good God, McCall," Smalls moaned dejectedly, rubbing his head, "You speak of, of Puff, as though she is the-----cat in the hat."

"Once more, Chief Smalls, Puff is the pet of a family acquaintance and there is nothing more to make of it."

"So you're willing to accept that the sight of a simple, little pet cat was enough to induce severe trauma in your son?"

McCall's shoulders sagged. "No, I don't truly accept that, but my wife wants me to believe it. Her and Miss Putnam."

"And just who the hell is this Putnam dame?"

"Nurse at the hospital. She and my wife have concocted this little theory that the reason my son is in trauma is because of his psychological love and desire to own Puff." McCall shrugged. "According to them, this is the cause of Aaron's torment."

"Have you seen the cat?"

"A strikingly magnificent creature."

"Yellow?"

"Yes."

On his way to the bar, Smalls stoked the fire, turning the burning embers over as flames crackled over them, making the stone hearth glow. "Tell me about this yellow cat."

"Puff," McCall corrected. Her name is Puff, and I've only see her twice, but the second time was weird. I wanted to call you, then."

"But you didn't, though. Why?"

Meg convinced me not to. Said I would look stupid if I told you what I had witnessed Puff do."

Unconcealed excitement flushed Smalls' face, but he tried to act calm. "What, if anything, did you see the yellow cat do?"

"*Puff!*" McCall replied stubbornly. "I saw *Puff* run like the wind." He spoke with awe. "Nothing, and I mean nothing should be able to move that fast." He glanced at Smalls. "She was like a flash of lightning. One second she was in one place and the next, she was some place else, and all that was left between point A and point B was a yellow blur. Trust me, I had never seen anything like it before. It was awesome."

"*And you thought I wouldn't be interested.*" Calming down, Smalls continued. "It's all water under the bridge now, but that info could very well have saved lives." He glared at McCall. "So, according to what you personally know to be true, yellow cat, er, Puff is endowed with some sort of super speed.?"

"I swear it."

By now, Smalls was shaking with excitement, his palms sweaty. "Tell me about the owner of the cat."

"There isn't much to tell actually. My family and I met Roscoe at the ribbon-cutting ceremony in First Ward, and my kids instantly fell in love with Puff, and my daughter charmed Roscoe into giving us a tour of what the neighborhood looked like when he lived there in the 50s and 60s."

Smalls flopped back in his chair. "What? He lived there in the 60s."

Roscoe had been forced to out of First Ward in 1964---"

"Oh my God," Smalls wailed over and over, clutching his head with one hand while nursing his drink in the other. His eyes rolled wildly in his head. "Everything fits."

"Is that good or bad?"

"We'll worry about that later." Smalls went to get another drink. "Tell me more about Roscoe."

"He's the janitor at the bank where I work. I got him the job. He comes in every evening."

"Boy-oh-boy-oh-boy," Small chanted. Then he grew serious. "Can I trust you?"

"Yes."

"Good, because I'm going to require your help." He took a sip of his drink. "I don't know what to make of Roscoe, but I know that Puff is a killer."

McCall's mouth opened to protest, but he was silenced by a curt wave of the police chief's hand.

"The reason you or no one has even heard of the murders in First Ward is because it was part of my plan to avoid public hysteria, but the killings did happen and they were brutally gruesome."

"And you think Puff did it? My God, why?"

"I'm not certain about why, but it has everything to do with the land. Puff, probably under the direction of Roscoe, feels First Ward belongs to them. Probably felt cheated when he was forced to leave in 64."

"So, he waits some thirty years later to do something about it?"

Smalls winced. "This is not the first time."

"*What!?*" McCall gasped. "This has happened before and you didn't stop it?'

"The first time was in 1964, immediately after all the black families were moved out of the neighborhood. I wasn't around then, but I had a talk with the man who ran the investigation, and he informed me that the events and murders now were identical, copy-cat replicas of the earlier ones."

"Well, shouldn't that man be here now helping resolve the issue?"

Smalls lowered his voice. "That man, Seth Jacobs, is dead. He was a victim of the slaughter this time. When we discovered the body, it was badly dismembered, but in his hand was a message." Smalls licked his lips. "The note said the same thing your son said."

"Yellow Cat?"

"Precisely."

"But how can Puff, so harmless----"

"Mr. McCall,…. How can I put this? *Puff is dead!*

McCall bolted upright in his chair. "Dead! Oh no, anything but dead, Chief Smalls. I have petted that damned cat."

"Relax," Smalls offered, "please. I estimate that Puff originally died-----."

"No! No! No!" McCall echoed in disbelief. "No!"

Smalls was patient. "As I was saying, the cat died in 1964." When there was no further outburst from McCall, the police chief resumed talking. "I even know where she was buried." He cast a glance at

McCall out of the side of is eyes. "Maybe you would like to visit the gravesite."

"No, that won't be necessary," McCall replied woefully, "but please continue."

"During the fall of 64 when the construction crews started razing the old houses, they also had to clear some land out back and when they did, they disturbed Puff's grave. A construction worker was killed instantly." Smalls gazed at his guest. "Guess what two words the man screamed continually as he was being mauled to death? Go ahead," Smalls prodded, "take a guess. What do you think that construction worker's last words were?"

"Yellow Cat."

Smalls nodded slowly. "Later that same evening, a CMPD police officer made contact with something that literally ate him alive, but just before the creature struck, the police officer made one final dispatch. Know what he transmitted?"

McCall nodded. He knew.

"Your son was lucky. As a matter of fact, your whole family is lucky since it is evident that the cat was in your home."

McCall trembled uncontrollably. "How can I help?"

"You have got to buddy up with Roscoe since you view him as a family friend. Hell, McCall, this is war so you get whatever you can get however you can."

"I-I don't know if I should do anything that might expose my family to any greater danger. Plus, I don't think I'm cut out for any of that cloak-and-dagger operation especially when my family is already up to our eyeballs in danger." McCall's fear was apparent. "I-I don't want to do anything that could get my family wiped out." McCall gripped his head between his sweaty hands. "I can't do it."

Smalls chose his next word carefully. "Please, no mistakes."

CHAPTER SIX

December hailed in on the tailwind of a fierce rainstorm that had brewed up from deep in the Atlantic, and had blown up the coast, splashing early morning Charlotte with heavy rains which by mid-morning had tapered to an annoying drizzle.

Smalls ducked into the doorway of Ruby Tuesday, shaking the rainy chill off him like he was a wet dog. He stood in the foyer for a second allowing his eyes to adjust and then stared into the vast, cavernous expanse of the restaurant, looking.

"Police Chief Smalls?"

The police chief answered the waitress who stood at his elbow. "Yes."

The waitress pointed. "Over there."

Smalls gingerly picked his way through the lunch-time crowd and found himself a seat across from a grey-haired, scholarly-looking black gentleman. Smalls offered his hand in greeting. "I'm Chief Smalls, so very honored you could make it."

"I'm Edward Marshall." The men shook hands warmly. "Bill McCoy said it was urgent." The brown-skinned man studied his white dinner companion. "How do you know Billy?"

"Well, actually, I don't, but it came to my attention that he was head of the Urban Institute over at UNCC, and that he had participated in the studies involved to redevelop blighted, urban, inner-city neighborhoods." Smalls made a bridge with his fingers and as he intently peered over them, he spoke with firmness. "Are you safe?"

"I've been sworn to absolute secrecy, if that's what you mean. Mr. Smalls, and I have every intention of honoring the oath, so you can speak freely, or as you white cats say, let it all hang out."

"Here's the deal," Smalls cracked rudely. "In the trunk of my car, I have all the info you need to give you the background of what's going on. I have outlined everything myself, and you will find maps, personal notes of mine, classified police reports, as well as the profile of all the murders." Refusing to allow the man to respond, Smalls ignored the questioning expression on Marshall's face. "Once you read the case history, you will be up to speed on this case. You can study these documents in private, and I'll call you within twenty-four hours to ask for your assessment and the return of the files."

" Marshall opened the restaurant's menu, studying the vegetarian entrees. "When do I get the chance to see the files?"

"As soon as you finish your veggies."

At 1300 hours, the phone rang and Smalls knew precisely who the caller was.

"Did you read?"

"Yes."

"Did you understand?"

"Yes."

"Do you have a solution?"

"Yes."

"Okay," Smalls commented casually, "what is it?"

"Go to hell."

"Huh?!"

"You heard me right. *Go to hell!* If what you suggest is true, and that only white people are catching it, then I find myself totally detached."

"Listen here, you prejudiced moron," Smalls snorted derisively, "you're committed."

"Like hell I am. I'm committed to keeping my dammed mouth shut and I will do exactly that, but I'm not, in the least, committed to any plan of action."

"Marshall, dammit, I'm warning you."

"I don't scare easily. Your briefcase, by the way, is at my office, and I have instructed my secretary to deliver it to you, provided you can present proper identification."

"Where's your fucking compassion, Marshall?"

"With my people. I don't have a beef with Puff as long as she continues to have a taste for white meat. Good day, Rambo."

The invitation carried with it the suggestion of seduction and both had sat throughout the private, candle-lit dinner immersed in the possibility of what could happen next. The sparkle in each other's eyes had given them a heated sense of knowing; of hoping.

By the time the meal was complete, both intuitively knew that a simple good-night kiss would be a pitifully shameful way to end the evening. Something bigger---better---was more appropriate.

The pair, caught up in the flickering swoon of candlelight and roses, intrigued by small talk and bubbling champagne, became more intent, with each passing breath, to solve the riddle of what to do with each other.

First, a smile, twinkling like stardust.

Next, a touch; the electricity of desire.

Then they were ready for something more.

"This is so unusual," the woman said softly, "so if I seem overly bold----."

"It is deliciously welcomed," Roscoe whispered in her ear.

On top of everything else the night promised, Roscoe and Elaine never permitted a single caress to be squandered or carelessly mishandled. They sensuously presided over each kiss, christening each moan with a unique pleasure all its own. Everything was tried and practiced except restraint, and when the last of foreplay's joys had been savored, they happily attended to the deeper needs of the flesh. The night was made for memories.

Puff was angry!

She reared on her trembling hind legs and searched for his scent and after a brief moment, molecules of his body chemistry floated on the breeze, but the aroma was tainted. Not his, alone. Puff screwed up her nose. The scent had come to her mingled, soiled.

Puff was angrier!

She followed her nose, plunging deeper into the immense whirlwind of the tarnished blackness that towered over the city. She flung herself through the bowels of the night, moving fast, becoming glacier. She was primed to kill.

Behind a row of brick-red apartments, she ran down a steep decline into a gutted ravine where dirty water dashed over moss-covered stones. She sipped daintily, flicking the water with her tongue. Sated, she traversed the slippery edge of the creek to the mouth where jagged rocks and twisted branches overhung the lip of the culvert. She leaped in, swimming powerfully into the reservoir.

Shaking herself dry, she slinked across the highway, ignoring the oncoming traffic. Cars bore down upon her, illuminating her eyes in their headlights, but none slowed or stopped. A man in a silver truck blew his horn. He swerved, switching lanes

"Stupid cat!" the hillbilly in the van muttered,

"Run over his fucking ass," his red-neck friend taunted.

Hillbilly Joe gave the van more gas. "Eat asphalt, you yellow mother---."

Suddenly, the van was spinning through the air, tumbling down the embankment, splashing nosily into the reservoir. How strange,

Hillbilly Joe and his red-neck friend thought. That fucking cat had just swatted their van like it was a speck of dust and now here they were.......underwater.

Puff, meanwhile, under another car, ripped through the A frame and bit the driver's neck which dangled limply on the man's shoulder as the car plowed into the ass-end of a tractor-trailer, bursting into spectacular flames.

The cat darted into the trees on the other side of I-77.

Elsewhere, it was the moment after. Roscoe's warm tongue investigated the shallow recesses of Elaine's soft navel. She moaned, holding his head.

Puff entered the neighborhood.

MEOW!

She strolled in front of the neat, tidy house, the forsythia and begonia plants long dead, ambushed by the chill of fall.

Instinctively, Roscoe drank in the foreboding menace that now accompanied the night and knew that he had better hurry home. Puff was either restless.........or jealous!

Roscoe let himself out, so Elaine still rested upon the rumpled sheets, coaxing more pleasure out of her content body. Her gentle hands squeezed and caressed all her secret places, urging herself to moan. She executed joy upon herself.

She was pleased. Now, she needed to fix the dry lump in her throat, and figured that a shot of Alize would wet her whistle just fine. And she was right, but immediately after downing the drink, she decided to check the mail she had left on the kitchen counter for later inspection. Walking towards the kitchen, she had a change of heart and did an about-face which set en route back to her bedroom.

When she got back to the bedroom, she gasped involuntarily; startled. She instinctively clutched her heart. A yellow cat was curled up on the carpet, playing with a spool of bright, red ribbon. Where did the cat come from?

Ignoring the animal, her heart still fluttering, she checked the windows. They were closed. She then marched out of the bedroom to check the doors. They were securely locked, so how did the cat get in?

Upon re-entering the bedroom, she pointed her finger at the cat, scolding the animal. "I'm sorry, kitty-cat, but I do not have the time or the temperament to play with you so you have got to go. *Shoo!*

Puff hissed at her, running under the bed, then under a chair, then, finally back under the bed.

"Dammit, cat. I don't feel like playing games and I'm not chasing you all over this house either." She stooped, extending her hand. Puff scooted farther under the bed, hiding in a distant corner. "Okay," Elaine snarled, "so it's going to be like that, huh?" Quicker than she had moved in a long time, she retrieved a long-handled, straw broom from the hall closet. She bent over. "Now, this is how I do it." She swept the brushy part of the broom under the bed angrily, poking forcefully in the darkened corner at the yellow-green eyes.

She felt resistance, heard the cat spit, and then experienced the almost unbearable lightness of the broom. She withdrew only a blue stick. Strangely, the bottom part was missing as if it had been sawed through, and Elaine pondered this although not for long because the big, comfortable, queen-sized bed was upended and slammed into the dresser over against the far wall.

Now, there was growling: the car. There, also, was screaming: her. Both sounds were agonizing, but of the two, only one, Elaine, got the notion that her time was at hand.

How right she was.

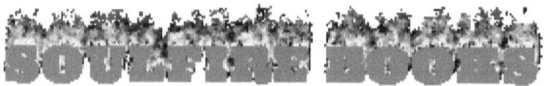

The phone was ringing off the hook.

It was nearly two o'clock in the morning, and Marshall had no idea who it could be, so he removed the bedside phone from its cradle reluctantly.

"Yes," he croaked, his voice choked with sleep. "Who is this?"

"It's me, you bastard," Smalls grunted. "I have sent a squad car to pick you up, so get dressed. I think you will want to see this for yourself."

"Smalls, are you insane?" Marshall huffed. "What's the meaning of this?"

"Dark meat, you asshole. Dark meat. Now, get dressed."

Twenty minutes later, the squad car exited off WT Harris Boulevard and skidded to an abrupt halt in front of a large Tudor style brick home. Marshall was ushered under the yellow crime scene tape, and into the house, passing a handful of police officers busy searching for clues. Inside the front door, Smalls waited. A portly black man, visibly shaken, stood near him, his face contorted with anguish.

"Come," Smalls said firmly.

Marshall followed, saying nothing. They entered the master bedroom.

"I'll be outside in the hallway," Smalls snapped. "I want you to get a good look at what Puff can do." He stopped in the doorway. "From the looks of things, she is not prejudiced, after all."

This was not to his liking at all, and the sight of death sickened Marshal. It was so undeniably brutal in its harshness. The top part of the body, her hair, her eyes, her face appeared so composed, so undisturbed, but below her waist, there was emptiness, an ugly gaping void where her womanhood should have been. That part of her had been torn out as if someone or something had dipped in and then had violently scooped it out.

Marshall jammed his fist into his mouth to quell the nausea. He took a few quick huffs of air and slowly the need to vomit subsided as the churning vortex sagged down deeper into his lower intestines. Shortly, thereafter, he rejoined Smalls in the hallway.

"Well, what do you think now?"

After a pause. "How do you know it was you know who?"

Smalls glared at Marshall angrily. "Because it fits the M.O."

"That's it. It's fit the pattern. Nothing more?"

"Okay, okay," Smalls conceded. "This one, she was a fighter; she battled back." He reached into his coat pocket. "Look at these." He held out a clear plastic bag. "See those yellow fibers. Cat hairs, and I have every reason to suspect they belong to you know who."

"Figures."

"Listen, Marshall, you in or you out?"

The delayed response unnerved Smalls. "I'm going to walk down the hallway to the bathroom and I'm going to take a piss. While I'm gone, think real hard about if you in or if you out."

The police chief's call to nature was unmercifully short, and when he had finished, he walked back into hallway, his hands stuffed deeply within the pockets of his coat. When he was as close as he could get to Marshall without violating his private space, he leaned in close before whispering. "You saw what I saw."

Marshall hugged himself. "I'm in," he said, "just don't start playing hero ad get me killed."

CHAPTER SEVEN

Smalls studied the EPA report again. It had been issued in 1963 and confirmed his suspicions. The area in First Ward bordering the creek had an unusually high level of toxicity and due to this, the Agency had ordered the area sealed off and enclosed. That was as far as it had gone, though. Inspectors had never notified the neighborhood that the ground and creek were contaminated. No one had ever thought to erect a fence or too put up a warning sign, and no one ever checked to see if the little, white building, the venetian blind company, ever stopped dumping waste in the creek.

And Puff was buried in that creek!

Amped up by that tidbit of info, Smalls conjectured that the creek was nothing more than a toxic chemical cocktail, but maybe, just maybe it was this toxicity that gave Puff her power. That had to be it. There was no other possibility. At least none that could withstand rational scrutiny of any kind. Even though, the EPA report had not specifically listed the names of the pollutants that were dumped in the creek and the surrounding area, it had mentioned that they were of a highly toxic nature.

He would put Marshall on that right away. If he could come up with the EPA report so easily, he could, more than likely, find out what all the active ingredients were that made up the toxic soup that the workers had dumped in the creek on a daily basis. Smalls hoped he once he learned the volatile character of these poisons, he would be able to determine which, if any, contributed to Puff's supercat capabilities.

Other than that, there was still the mystery of Roscoe. What was he, really? Was he capable of immense destructive fury the same as his pet. Had he killed, would he? Smalls didn't know----yet. What he did know was that Roscoe had been intimately involved with Elaine Paige, the woman found disemboweled last week. Who had killed her, the man or the cat?

The cat!?

Was jealousy too far-fetched a notion? Smalls was not beyond that line of thinking since he heard of instances where house pets became extremely upset with the arrival of a new baby in the house. As a matter of fact, he had just read where either Rikki Lake or Jenny Jones had to get rid of a beloved dog because the animal had acted aggressively towards her newborn baby. Surely, a clear case of pet jealousy? Smalls could buy that. Maybe Puff wanted Roscoe's undivided attention. Smalls smiled. After all, the cat had come all the way back from the dead.

The phone rang.

It was Marshall. "I did a roll call on all the stuff that was dumped at the site, and it turns out that they were basically solvents of one type or another. Pretty hazardous stuff in terms of causing allergies and respiratory problems after prolonged exposure."

"But nothing to induce supernatural powers?"

"Think about it, Smalls," Marshall cracked, "do you think they'd publish it. That would be top-secret because they would be spoon-feeding the soldiers that shit before sending them off to war."

Smalls groaned pitifully. "A lot of good this does me?"

"Well, once this shit is over with this cat, I intend to file a lawsuit against the company for knowingly dumping toxic waste in an occupied neighborhood, and then sue the EPA for knowingly permitting another neighborhood to be built on top of a hazardous dump site. There is no telling how many black families are out there right now suffering debilitating neurological disorders due to this environmental racism."

"Hold on!" Smalls yelped. "Hold on a fucking minute. That's all fine and dandy if you want to go after the EPA and whoever the hell else ruffles your feathers, but don't switch horses on me in the middle of the stream. We need to stay focused, okay. This is about a cat."

Puff.

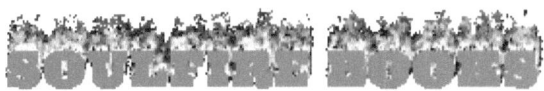

The day was done and Roscoe silently returned home. He wanted a woman, but stole a sidelong glance at Puff and decided against the notion. He could wait.

No sooner had the cat gotten out of the car than she ran to the front door of the apartment meowing wildly, rubbing her nose against the cold bricks. Abruptly, the meows turned caustic, deepening into a growl.

Roscoe watched.

Puff marched back and forth across the porch, moving carefully, making no sound. She lifted each paw high, suspended it, then lowered it into a tiny, silent stomp as though there was something underneath that needed to be crushed. Puff was agitated.

Finally, the yellow cat stretched and Roscoe could see the power rippling through her body. She started to make clicking sounds with her tongue and then leaped into the air, taut and tense. Next, she ran off.

Roscoe shrugged, went into the apartment.

Out of habit, Puff crossed the busy street swiftly and using her nose like a compass, looped around the boulevard heading towards the perimeter of uptown. Off to her side, near Parker Heights, she stopped twice. Heavy noise. She ignored the commotion, checked the wind to get her bearings straight and then forged ahead.

At the traffic intersection near The Town & Country Drive-Thru. She picked up the pungent odor of fish and cats. She skirted under the fence and approached from the rear where several cats were busy feasting on scraps of greasy fish they had managed to salvage from a trash can.

To her left of this alpha group was a small contingent of hungry kittens huddled together, waiting for the big cats to finish eating so they could devour what little might be left.

A huge Tom cat faced Puff. He was the leader and emitted a low, vicious growl, passing menacingly in front of Puff. The tom cat's body was tense, its claws unsheathed and bared. He sniffed at Puff, but nothing. He approached Puff at an angle, moving to her rear. Puff stood totally motionless. The big, grey cat sniffed again, only more deeply this time. Still, his nose detected nothing.

By now, the others perceived a threat and stopped eating. They advanced on Puff as a single unit. Another tom, overweight and balding cat, stood nose-to-nose with Puff, nudging the yellow cat's head from side to side. He was trying her.

The other cats settled back, pawing the ground and poking their noses at Puff in disdain. A fight was inevitable. The lead cat circled to Puff's right, and in sudden swift movement, his paw shot forth as quickly as lightning, aiming to tear a patch out of the yellow cat's flank, but he grossly miscalculated. Consequently, he never saw it coming, never knew what hit him so there was no way to protect himself. A gashing red stream of blood splashed out of the concave hollow in his chest. His abdomen was ripped open and red, hot blood poured on the ground like steaming emollients, warming the asphalt.

The balding, fat cat's luck wasn't much better because in a terrifyingly blinding instant, Puff had curled inward, curving to the right, striking at the cat's ears and the swollen, fat head rolled onto the ground. The cat's empty shoulders twitched spasmodically until death laid him down on his side, but even after this, blood continued to ooze from the festering wound.

The remaining big cats vanished, but the kittens, too frightened to move, watched Puff warily. Puff purred maternally, bathing the babies with reassurance as she stepped over the aluminum trash can and then slashed at the metal with her claw. Scraps of fish wiggled out of the opening, providing a veritable feast for the young ones. Satisfied, Puff darted into the traffic.

Her legs were tired by the time she reached Hawthorne Park, but the scent was stronger now, arriving through the wind with the stench of bourbon. Puff wrinkled her nose in disgust, moving up Pecan Avenue until she had identified exactly where the man was. She passed under two parked cars, emerged across the street, and cautiously waited by the front door of Anntony's Caribbean Café.

She waited.

And waited.

Fifteen minutes later, the hair on the back of her neck stood erect. A man, black and intoxicated, approached, pushing through the exit door.

"MEOW!"

Puff crossed his path, her back arched. She hissed.

The man stopped abruptly, staring, wondering; hoping not. "Nice kitty," he croaked, his eyes bulging. He stepped around the yellow cat, his heart beating dangerously fast as the animal rubbed timidly against his leg, letting him past.

"Thank Jesus," Marshall gasped, clutching is chest. "Whew, for a moment I thought that was......"He fell silent, not wanting to even mention the name to himself. Now that he was clear of the menace, he whistled as he crossed the street to his car, but still glanced around for the cat. He smiled. The poor thing had probably followed someone home.

In the parking lot behind the Stanly Drugstore, he buried his hand into his Styrofoam carry-out tray and dug out a fat, jumbo shrimp. He popped it into his mouth, crunching it between his teeth, savoring the flowing succulent juices. At his car, he shuffled the tray to his left hand and fished in his pockets for his keys.

"Oh, God, no!"

The yellow cat was perched atop the roof of his car.

"*NO!*" he screamed again. "HELP!" He ran around into the light in front of the drugstore. "*HELP!*" He glanced behind him but there was no sign of the cat. "Thank you, Jesus," Marshall prayed happily. For a change, good luck. In the near distance, crossing Hawthorne, approaching him was a police car. Marshall almost went limp with relief. He waved his hands frantically to signal the cop as he continued to run down the sidewalk, his eyes glued to the cruising patrol car. He waved both arms more desperately as the police car turned onto the premises at the far end of the strip mall. He damned near screamed for joy.

The yellow cat came crashing through the interior wall of Roy White's Flower Shop, and before she hit the ground, Marshall was left standing there, a wide, bugged-eyed look of horror on his face. The cat had run off with his heart. He had just enough time to figure everything out before he dropped dead.

Puff literally vanished. That's how fast she was running.

Smalls didn't recognize the officer's name so he spent the first twenty minutes going over the man's file. He wished to develop, or at least try to get a feel for the type of human he was dealing with. Overall, Elliot Webster was a good cop. Intelligent. Dedicated. Sane.

Now, he was ready to go on with the interview. "Send him in,"

Elliot Webster was new to the force; only two years. He was tall and thin with hair that was longer than most of the other officers in the department.

"Have a seat, Officer Webster."

He did. "Thank you.

"Your record is impeccable," Smalls offered. "Keep up the good work." His voice changed. "Tell me what happened at the flower shop. Take your time."

"Well sir, I was in my immediate patrol sector and at around 2100 hours, I turned into the parking lot where Stanly Drugstore's is located, but I was at the bottom end."

"Is that the end where the flower shop is?"

"Yes sir, that is correct. Stanly is on one end and Roy's is on the other." Webster paused. "Coming up near the entrance of the building, I immediately recognized a black male attempting to get my attention."

"How so?"

"He was waving his arms over his head frantically, you know, in the typical distress flagging motion. Anyway, he was running towards me, the car."

"Did you see anyone or anything chasing him?"

"Negative, sir. He was simply running, but he did appear to be attempting to flee from someone."

"Or something?"

"Something, sir?"

"A dog, perhaps?"

"I get your point, sir, but there was no dog, and my visibility was 100 percent."

"Then how do you explain seeing the man getting his heart ripped out, and then not seeing who or what did it?"

"Sir, I never reported that I saw the man getting his heart torn out. I never even reported that I even witnessed him being attacked. What I conveyed was that I saw a black male running and that I saw the front window of the flower shop shatter. I also relayed that it was my initial impression that the black male had broken the window."

"Why would you think that, Officer?"

"It's winter, sir. I felt he might possibly have been a vagrant who was cold and wanted to make sure he went to jail where it would be warm. Also food. It happens a lot."

"What changed your mind?"

"First of all, he was too well-dressed to be a homeless person."

"Anything else?"

"Yes sir," the officer wheezed, "the man had no fucking heart. Excuse the profanity, sir, but something invisible had snatched his heart clean from his chest."

"Why do you say......invisible?"

Webster swallowed. "Because I didn't see a fucking thing, sir, and I was looking right at him."

"Could it have been---?"

"No sir."

"But you didn't know what I was going to say."

"It didn't matter, Chief. All I know is that it could have only been what it is." He stared at Smalls. "And it was invisible."

"I believe you, Officer Webster. I was simply hoping there was something more."

"Trust me, sir, that's all there was except for a brief bright yellow flash."

"*Yellow flash?!*"

"Yes sir."

"And you saw it?"

"Yes sir."

"That's all for now. You're dismissed."

CHAPTER EIGHT

The shit had hit the fan!

To Smalls, the death of Marshall was a heart-to-heart ultimatum, a non-apologetic, eye-opening, kiss-my-ass indictment. The police Chief thought of McCall, then himself. If what had happened to Marshall was a preview......he shuddered at the thought.

He wanted to call McCall, but he wasn't eager to scare the living daylights out of the man. Anyway, what would he say to reassure the banker? 'Oh, it's okay, Clinton. Let's wait and see what Puff does next.' Smalls groaned miserably. He already knew what would happen next. One or the other of them would die. It was that simple. It was that simple because they were the only ones left.

His mind wouldn't allow him to focus. He was really afraid and there was a tremendous congestion in his chest as his heart did a lot of loud banging under his shirt. It was almost as if he were experiencing cardiac arrest, but he didn't do anything to save himself. He merely sat immobile, grimacing in pain, staring at his empty hands. Hell, he wanted to die. Congenital heart failure would be a whole hell of a lot better than what he could expect from the brutal, savage yellow cat.

Unfortunately, the morbid moment was whisked away as suddenly as it had come and all he was left with was a squeamish churning in the pit of his belly. He would live. He gazed solemnly at the ceiling, unsure of whether to curse or to pray. He decided to do neither. He simply looked at his feet.

Underneath it all, he did still feel afraid and it was a robust, full-bodied fear and in the glow of this newly-discovered dread, he suddenly realized, in a bizarre way, how priceless everything now seemed to be. All of a sudden, every artifact, every object in his home gleamed like a treasure. Everything appeared touched with a special sentimental badge of identification. The chair he sat in, for instance, was a valuable relic, given him by a loving uncle. The lamp in the corner, memorabilia from a long lost love affair.

A tear fell from his eye and he dabbed at it with a silk handkerchief that had belonged to his son. He stared at the exquisite monogram---BTS---and another tear dropped, but he brushed it away only to peer at the colorful globe which had been a gift from a grandchild.

The whole house reeked with personal touches, either his or someone he loved. He gave himself a tour. In the salon, there was richness, 14th century elegance where a leather-crafted couch and a quad of wig-backed chairs enclosed a coffee table inlaid with crystal. The rug was Victorian.

He could go no further. So much he had taken for granted, so much he had assumed and/or had gotten used to. Now, thanks to last night's death of a man he scarcely knew had pushed him to the other extreme. Suddenly, he wished for the chance to relearn how to appreciate life. Was there still time? The tears started again, and he felt alone and scared. He would have to take a Valium soon. But first, he had to induce logical thinking which would be critical to his chances of survival. Okay, whom did he attack? The man? Or the cat? And just how did he attack Puff when the animal was seemingly indestructible? Could he even destroy Roscoe?

He carefully studied the file on Roscoe. It was only a snapshot, but it was all he had. Roscoe Brown had been born in the 50s at Good Samaritan Hospital and had spent all of his youth in First Ward on Sixth Street. As a child, he didn't play well with other children and since he was painfully shy and withdrawn, he took refuge in books. He seemed to dislike playing games and he very seldom laughed or smiled. Most of the grownups felt he was much too serious for his age.

It was around 1963, it seemed, that someone had given the sad, young boy a bright, yellow kitten. Puff. He and the cat went everywhere together and a lot of people actually believed that Roscoe and the cat were so close that they could communicate. The few who didn't absolutely believe this, never doubted it.

When the cat had died, everyone on Sixth Street had remembered that also. It had destroyed Roscoe. He shrank. Everyone also knew where Roscoe had buried the cat.

In 1964, Roscoe and his family had moved to Piedmont Courts on Tenth and Seigle. Right afterwards, the First Ward neighborhood was demolished. Instantly, the brutal slasher killings had commenced, the trail of bodies leading to Piedmont Courts before going completely dead. This time the trail of blood had led to Dalton Village where Roscoe now lived, and the same thing that had sparked the killings thirty-three years ago had set them off this time-----the razing of that neighborhood.

First Ward. Roscoe. Puff. 1964. Piedmont Courts
Earle Village. Roscoe. Puff. 1997. Dalton Village
Murder!

These were the pieces to this horrible puzzle, and now, at long last, Smalls knew how to make them fit. He just didn't know what to do too dispose of the frightening image he had put together.

From time to time, Smalls vacillated in his beliefs as to if or not Roscoe played the role of some Dark Avenger. On some rare occasions, he was certain of it, but, at other times, dismissed the notion as silly. Right now, he was sure of it.

The more he studied the notes on the accounts of the murders and deaths that had occurred in First Ward and Earle Village, he was a becoming more comfortable with the idea that Roscoe was indeed the deadly author of some of the slayings.

It was Roscoe that he would go after.

"Damn," Smalls yelled out in anguish. "Damn!"

Friday, December 12th.

Over the last few months, it had almost become a neighborhood tradition and this week would be no exception. Those folks were—well--looney. Therefore, the cops had to do what was best for the city which meant that every Friday evening, they barricaded First Ward. After, precisely, five o'clock, the entire community would be sealed completely off until Monday morning, and if you weren't a cop or a medic, you couldn't get in---or out.

It was like the neighborhood had a curse on it, and the residents, all of them, acted as if they were under some sort of spell. Friday night just seemed to bring out the devil in them because just as soon as the lawyers, doctors, business leaders, etc. arrived home from work on Friday, they would commence to raising hell. They called it celebrating, but the police called it lawlessness, and that was the reason why they worked round-the-clock in First Ward every weekend.

The phenomenon was disquieting and puzzling to everyone except Smalls. He understood clearly, but he was the only one. During the week, the residents of First Ward were honest, hard-working civic leaders and captains of industry, but quitting time on Friday is what they loved most. You could spot most of them even before they got home. They were usually the wild-eyed ones, dodging in and out of rush hour traffic like speeding daredevils. Can't wait to get home to raise hell. Speeding through the city streets, they, more than likely, would have their car stereo blasting either one or the other of their favorite songs: "Living For The Weekend" by The O'jays, or Elton's John's, "Friday Night All Right For Fighting."

In a luxurious townhouse off Fifth Street, the five men lounging around in their smoking jackets and Italian slippers were greatly upset. They stared is shock at the appearance of their esteemed colleague, Dr. Axelrod Edminsten. He had offended the elegant sensibilities of these highly-refined gentlemen and they were appalled at the breach in etiquette. Thaddeus Motley was the first to address the issue.

"What up, dawg? Why you disrespecting the crib by coming up in here without the proper gear?"

"Yeah, homes, you know you can't get down," another colleague added, "if your attire ain't straight.'

"So, what up, G" the philosophy professor asked stoically.

Dr. Edminsten huffed. "Let me check y'all lames. Personally, I ain't with the dress code no more."

"So, that's how you bringing it?" Motley stood up. "This me, baby. This me, Dr. T. I'm the one who brought you in the group when didn't nobody else dig you 'cause you ain't have but two, funky-assed degrees. I went against my partners for you, and this is the thanks I get,"

"That's how it be sometimes," Edminsten snorted. "You gonna pass me that fucking stem or what?"

"Hold up, motherfucker, not so quick. You come in here like my crib some penny-ante, run-of-the-mill crack house. Look around you. Where else motherfuckers be smoking out of crystal stems, or be chopping they shit up on fine silver? We got class in this spot, you ungrateful slob."

Edminsten flexed his shoulders. He peeled back his Hilfinger jacket, exposing the butt of his 9mm. "I can pay the cost to be the boss." He wiggled his fingers like a gunslinger, getting ready to draw. "Go for what you know, chump."

Motley stepped out from behind the desk, his eyes cold. "You ain't said nothing but a thang." He shrugged his shoulders and the red, silk jacket slid delicately to the floor. A Glock was stuffed in the waistband of his French-cuffed trousers. "Let's get busy."

When the smoke cleared, both men laid upon the expensive Persian rug, bleeding profusely.

And that was only the beginning. Two and a half blocks down the street.

"Open this door, bitch" the man yelled, "you know it's my turn tonight."

"Stop acting like a sucker," the woman shouted back through the door.

"That's a'ight, ho. If I get up in there, y'all gonna be the suckers, sucking on my 9."

"Go 'head on now, Timmy," a man's voice boomed through the door to the man outside, "You more of a ho than she is so run on home 'cause I ain't wanting to have to dust yo' ass off."

"Kiss my ass, Tommy. I'm gonna tell her husband."

"And if you do---"

"Then what?"

"Hold up," the woman screamed, "that's between you two motherfuckers. You know I can't tell y'all asses apart. That's what you get for being twins." The woman smirked. "One of y'all just as good as the other, so from now on, it's first come, first served."

"Tommy, you ain't shit."

"Yo' Mama."

Timmy started pleading. "Do she ne whupping that thang on you like she ain't got no sense?"

"Sho' do, lil brother, sho do."

"OMG!" Timmy groaned. "Do the no-good hussy let you do her like a dog?"

"Yep, and I be walking the dog with her motherfucking trifling ass."

"When-when y'all get through getting busy, do she make her coochie smoke a cigarette?"

"A motherfucking Newport 100."

"Man," Timmy ranted, "you better open that motherfuckinbg door and stop playing before I get stupid and get savage on both of y'all white asses."

The door opened.

"Timmy!"

"Tommy!"

The twins hugged each other warmly.

"Now, let's Georgia this stupid bitch."

And it was still early. Just around the corner.

"Hey you."

"Who, me?"

"Yeah, you, you little nerd."

"I must make it clear that my righteous name is Malik. I have denounced my former government name, Merle Nelson II.

Additionally, I feel compelled to address the issue of being referred to as a nerd. In my most humble opinion, it is disrespectful, and in my heart of hearts, I resent it immensely."

"Fuck you, nerd."

The three toughs laughed derisively, scowling.

Malik coughed. "It really upsets me when I'm misunderstood." He faced the bullies. "Has that ever happened to you? I must say that it sucks." The frail, bespectacled white teenager shrugged. "It means that I have failed. It means that as broad and as expansive as the English language is, I have failed in my most sincere attempt to reach into this wonderful maze of words to find just the right ones to make you motherfuckers know not to fuck with me." He whipped out a set of nunchaku, the martial arts fighting sticks, and a few seconds later, he casually strolled to the nearest police barricade. "I feel it most prudent that I inform you, kind sirs, that there are a trio of very injured men a few kilometers from where we now stand." Malik's eyes blazed with pride. "I fucked 'em up pretty bad."

The sergeant in duty looked at the paramedic. "Better get on over there. That's Malik, the martial arts expert. His M.O. is to dress up like a nerd, and stroll through the hood with his nose stuck in a book." The sergeant shook his head. "And what bunch of bullies can resist picking on a bookworm? Only thing is that Malik gets off on that kind of shit."

"What kind of hell-hole is this?" the paramedic asked.

"Not hell-hole," the sergeant corrected. "Hell."

L

CHAPTER NINE

Smalls knew it was going to happen even before he had gotten to the Mayor's office. Already, a full hour had passed and he still was no closer to seeing the Mayor than he had been yesterday, and he was beginning to fume inwardly. He had come today in person since he had not received an appropriate response to his phone calls, and now even that he had made his presence known, everyone was practically intent on acting out the charade that the Mayor was too busy to be disturbed.

"For starters," the Mayor's aide said brightly, "the Mayor wishes to thank you for your patience, Chief Smalls, but at the same time, regrets that he can't grant you an audience." The aide gestured expansively. "You can't imagine how busy this place is during the holidays." He chuckled. "Ho, ho, ho. Santa is on the way."

"And so is Puff."

"Puff? What does Puff, the magic dragon, have to do with Christmas?"

Smalls slowly rose to leave, then abandoned the concept. He plopped back down heavily as he propped his feet up on the highly polished desk.

The aide's eye grew wide. "Why, Chief Smalls," he sputtered, "what is the meaning of-----?"

"Shut up and listen," Smalls snapped, "we all might be dead before New Year's Day anyway."

"Chief Smalls, is it possible that you're over-worked, a little stressed out, perhaps. Just the same, your friend and mine, the Mayor is embroiled in the debate about the historic Park Elevator building, and then there is the husband and wife team from Chicago who wants the city to cough up $750,000 to cut a road on Freedom Drive so they can build a movie complex. How marvelous. And who do you think they called in to help lure the Minnesota Twins to Charlotte?"

"Who else, but----"

"You bet your ass, they did. The damned phone never stop ringing. Why, just the other day the former Mayor Harvey Gantt wanted advice from the Mayor about buying McDonald's Cafeteria over on Beatties Ford Road."

Smalls leaned close. "Pay attention. I want you to run and tell the Mayor that there is a killer cat on the loose in his wonderful city who has already slaughtered a number of his residents. This cat, Puff, by name, is no ordinary feline. This kitty has the power to tear men's heart right out of their chest, or to strip the meat off their bones with a few rakes of her razor-sharp claws. Oh yeah, please make sure the Mayor, your friend and mine, knows that the reason I can't kill the fucker is because she is already dead."

Starks looked perplexed, a confused look on his effeminate face. "How can you keep a straight face when you tell that tall tale?"

"Because, dammit, it's no laughing matter. Here, give him these. They're photos of the dead, all victims of Puff's fury. I was going to go it alone, but the city is under attack, and I need help. I think I just might go visit my friend, Dannye Romine-Powell, at The Observer and to spill my guts. At least, if nothing else, mass hysteria will evacuate the city, leaving Puff no one to murder."

Starks stared at the photos. "If this is true, then the last thing we need is public panic."

"You bet your ass, it's true."

"And just what kind of cat is Puff? A mountain lion? A panther? A-____?"

"Stop it, Starks," Smalls said firmly. Puff is a kitty-cat."

"*A kitty-cat!?*" Starks exploded. "And you expect me to believe that?" He thumbed through the gruesome pictures again. "That a fucking house cat is capable of this sort of awesome destruction. Smalls, you must be nuts. I was almost ready to go along with you at first, but you blew your own boat out of the water with this kitty-cat bullshit." He winked. "Come on, level with me, Smalls, what's really going on? What's the real scoop on these pics, you can tell me. Hell, if you want to play a little trick on the Mayor, hey, I won't say a mumbling word, but don't ask me to back you up with this killer kitty-cat shit. Wow."

"Ever since October," Small said finally, "this cat has been killing people. In the entire city, there are only a handful of individuals, mostly law enforcement types, who are even remotely aware of what has been going on. I went into this thinking I could stop it before it got too big to be noticed, but I was wrong. I made the fucking mistake of trying to spare the Mayor, your friend and mine, a gigantic headache, but what he needs to understand is that if Puff is not stopped soon, he won't have a city to mayor." Smalls stood to leave. "In my thirty years on the force, I have never once falsified or distorted any report of a crime." He placed his hands on Starks shoulders, pushing him farther down into his soft, comfortable leather chair. "Boy, if I ever tell you it's raining piss, then you best take my word." He released his grip. "Tell our friend, the Mayor, to expect my resignation."

It was December 19th, Friday noon, the last day of school before the Christmas vacation. Smalls flung the report away and dashed outside to his squad car, hurriedly jumping behind the wheel. He activated both lights and sirens. The precinct was just a few blocks from where he wanted, needed to be so he just might make it in time. He glanced at his watch. 12:03. That meant twelve minutes---and counting.

He barreled into First Ward, turning hard at Alexander Street and slammed on his brakes. *"Damn!"* he cursed, the car skidding. He couldn't proceed because the road that used to be there in 1964 no longer existed so he veered around the park. He peeked at his watch and grimaced. He'd lost precious minutes, but now he was on McDowell so he still had a chance. He sped past Little Rock Church, down the hill to Ninth, ignored the red light at the intersection, and zoomed up the backside of Tenth. He stepped on the gas and skidded to a halt at what should have been an intersection.

He cursed again. "Damn!" he muttered. "What gives?" He glared at the apartment building that now squatted where Alexander Street used to cross Ninth Street, and his mind flashed back to 1964. According to the report, it was here---right here—on the last day of school for the Christmas break that a very terrible, very tragic accident occurred. A girl....leaving school......coming home.....was struck by a car......and killed.

Smalls looked around him, then at his watch. 12:15. This was the time. This was the spot, but it couldn't happen here. No intersection. No way.

Suddenly, the sound of squalling brakes and squealing tires filled the air, and Smalls knew what the commotion was, so he just dropped his head and groaned. She—whoever she was—was dead. This little, white girl was just as dead as Mary Smith, the little, black girl, had been in 1964.

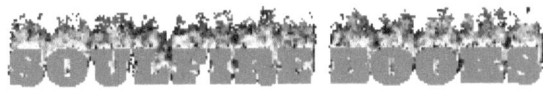

It had been another sleepless night. As a fact, Smalls hadn't slept in over three or four days. Or eaten. And he greeted each dawn the same way, wringing his hands and staring holes into the ceiling. Soon, his abused body would simply fail, stop working, and go bust. Plus, he was sure to die soon. Who was left? McCall? Himself?

He once believed he could make it to the first of the year, but now he wasn't so sure. He no longer possessed the audacity to believe in longevity. The yellow cat was just too powerful. He was a goner and he knew it. There was no inner strength to draw upon, no sweltering reserves of confidence to stroke his ego with, no civic pride. What there was---was nothingness.

This morning, in particular, was one where he was in no mood to be fucked with.

"Briefed you!? He shrieked hotly. "Evidently, he didn't brief you good enough because if he had, you would be scared shitless, your fucking eyes would be rolling around wildly in your head, and you sure as hell wouldn't be standing there with that sheepish grin on your face, looking like you just left the tanning salon. You would be whiter than milk." Smalls rubbed his hands across his heads nervously. "That's the kind of situation we have on our hands and everybody in this office as well as the city council are all rushing off to Spirit Square to listen to Handel's Messiah."

Harry Berkowitz frowned at Smalls. "Could we be a little more friendly? I'm not accustomed to be screamed at or scolded, and I don't intend to tolerate it despite the severe nature of this problem so tone down your vitriolic diatribe."

"And just who the hell are you?" Smalls shouted. "Another of the Mayor's errand boys? All I know is that you're not Bill Clinton, you're not a relative, and you damned sure don't look like a friend, so kiss my ass."

Berkowitz had seen the conditions before. "When was the last time you had some rest, Chief Smalls, or a decent meal." The tone was patient, concerned. "In your present state of near exhaustion, you're a menace to yourself so I suggest that get some R and R and we can resume our talks in a day or so."

Smalls laughed bitterly. "Is-is that what you think? You think we have a day or so to just relax and go fishing." He scowled, frowning at the man. "Who the hell are you just so I can report your incompetent ass?"

The man extended his hand. "I'm General Harry Berkowitz, US Army, on loan from the Strategic Defense Initiative."

"Star Wars?" Smalls asked hazily.

"Star War to some, SDI to us a headquarters." The men shook hands. "Glad to meet you, Chief Smalls."

"Star Wars," Smalls mumbled, visibly pleased. "I'll be damned." He clasped the General's hand warmly. "The fucking pleasure is all mine."

"Trust me, the Army has carefully studied the situation here with Puff and we're here to destroy her provided we can't successfully capture the animal. The government would love to study and examine this creature."

"You can take my word on this, sir. Puff, is by no means, an experimental type cat."

"Oh, I wouldn't be so sure of that so please don't think that your little kitty ranks that high on the Army's alarm meter. In no time, I'll have Puff afraid of mice." Berkowitz grinned. "If the cat proves to be a worthy opponent, which I seriously doubt, we still have a few toys left over from the cold war era that we are just dying to test."

For the next minute and a half, Smalls let the sudden euphoria sweep over him. The cavalry was here, and that was a good enough sign for him to once more plan for the future. There would be, after all, life after Puff. All of a sudden, he felt the joy of the season and he now felt more like Santa than Scrooge. At last, life was good again.

"Out in our test facility in New Mexico, we ran some prelims on the chemicals that you suspect were dumped at the spot where the cat was buried."

"We already did that."

"Yes, but with equipment and engineers only available for civilian use. It goes without saying that our Uncle Sam has a few unspecified gadgets that are light years ahead of their generic prototypes that are available to the general public." Berkowitz winked his eye. "You never give away your best toys. At any rate, other tests will be performed on the basis of what the preliminary ones suggest, and once our feasibility reports are analyzed against the background of what we already know and what we discover in the meantime, I think we'll understand the nature of the cat."

"So, no one at the Army is laughing?"

"Can't tell you much, but for quite a few decades a lot of high level army research has gone into UFOs and an alien invasion. We know a lot more than we admit publicly, but what is interesting is that of the few UFO crashes that we know of is how they left very highly saturated levels of toxicity in the ground surrounding the crash." The General chose his next words carefully. "It is suspected that some of these toxins could very well cause mutation and chromosomal aberrations on the order of turning the normal into the supernormal."

Smalls relaxed, relieved. He smiled warmly. "I'm glad that someone is finally getting serious."

"Excluding cops under your direct supervision, who else knows about Puff?"

"Just Clinton McCall and his family." Smalls fixed a stone-faced glare on the General. He politely cleared his throat. I know that cats, as such, are not capable of human reasoning. I mean, cats, usually, function from instinct and not intelligence, right? I mean I know this, but earlier this month, Puff committed a very uncharacteristic killing, so unlike any of the others from now or back in 64."

"What made it different?"

"The victim was black, a female." Smalls squirmed uneasily in the chair. This murder seemed to be an execution, more or less. A sexual execution to be exact."

Berkowitz's eyes widened.

"The woman was mutilated, had her vagina ripped out."

For the first time, the General stood. He was of medium height, but his stiffly erect carriage made him appear taller. He was remarkably distinguished-looking with a faint aura of southern gentility although he was a born and bred Yankee. His complexion was roughly the hue of tanned leather engraved with marble-sized clear, blue eyes. He was a good-looking soldier. He paced behind the desk before breaking into a wide grin. "Smalls, you're going to have me flipping burgers at a fast-food joint if we blow this case." He looked out of a window. "You make a case for that cat that I was not expecting." He turned to face Smalls. "In the space of a few minutes, we have gone from endowing this cat with intellectual and psychic powers to now awarding her the emotional capacity to experience jealousy."

"Not to mention the passion," Smalls added, "to act it out in a grossly human fashion-----murder!"

"I agree. Now, I want you out of here and somewhere asleep. It's a miracle you can see with your eyes that heavy-lidded. To be effective, you must be alert. Get some sleep, and that's an order."

CHAPTER TEN

On the evening of the day after Christmas, Roscoe propped the front door open and began packing the boxes into the U-Haul he had rented. He wanted to be completely settled into his new apartment by tomorrow night in time for the Hornets game.

He no longer felt safe in Dalton Village, so he found himself a place on Sunnyside Avenue. Deep down, he knew it was time to go and he saw no need to poke fun at his intuition or attempt to second guess his gut feelings. Plus, he didn't intend to become an easy target of Chief Smalls' plotting. The bastard. It had taken him a while to figure out exactly who Smalls was, but was only mildly surprised to learn he was so highly-motivated to pursue the happenings in First Ward. Now, he would put the Chief on the defensive.

He stowed the last box into the truck.

"Puff," he called. "Let's get the hell out of Dalton Village."

In the few additional minutes it had taken him to check to make sure he hadn't left anything behind, Roscoe turned as cold as ice. *He would kill! Tonight.* And he knew precisely where to strike. Driving swiftly across town, he turned into First Ward, wondering who stayed in the Sixth Street Alley by the old tree where he had gotten his first kiss. He sneered. The white folks shouldn't have moved there, destroying the sanctity of that memorable event. Now, someone would pay dearly for that transgression.

The evening wind coughed up trash that had spilled from a knocked-over trashcan, pushing the debris forward like tumbleweeds as billows of steam hissed evilly, rising eerily from out of the sewer grate as the magnificence of darkness paid strict attention to covering everything with black.

One of the townhouses on Sixth Street opened up, a man stumbling out, singing. Roscoe drove on. Such easy prey would not be honored tonight. He wanted whoever lived there---in the scared shadow of where he and Wilhemenia had kissed. Roscoe lowered his head in reverence of that moment, so long ago. That kiss had been special and had left him, a young boy, filled with an exotic excitement that had nothing to do with sex. Their relationship was too innocent and pure for that, but he had been awakened to the discovery that little girls possessed an erotic magic that was worth exploring.

When he looked up, inexpressible rage sizzled in his eyes. He sat upright and tall, seething with rabid indignation. How dare white folks trespass upon such fond memories? His anger roared, almost overwhelming him to the point where he felt the desire to torch the entire neighborhood, to scorch the earth until nothing remained but an ash-stricken garden where he could either plant his memories, or to repair his hurt.

But no.

He wasted no time kicking the door in and stepping across the threshold of the home, staring down the frightened family gathered around the television set. They seemed to shrink in his presence, to wither under his gaze. Then he emptied both guns. The mother dying in the arms of the father while junior took two shots to the head before toppling over where he sat, splattering the entertainment console with baby blood.

And just like that, he was finished.

Roscoe felt no compelling need to rush, so he casually wiped the guns clean and walked solemnly away. He stood in the yard…..in the same spot where he had kissed Wilhemenia. He gently laid the pair of guns down, touching the muzzles together as if they were kissing. How sweet, he thought.

Then he was gone. He had to light his first candle since this was the first night of Kwanza.

Chief Smalls wiped the sleep from his eyes. Man, he felt better. He stared at the phone and started to place the receiver back on its cradle, but decided not to. Not just yet. The same went for his beeper. It also would stay OFF until after he had shaved and eaten breakfast.

He flicked on the TV and found Denise Dory, so he decided to watch the morning news as the coffee brewed. The first images he saw were of local residents in Elizabeth who were upset over two planned condo projects slated for their neighborhood. Smalls watched, half-amused, then laughed aloud when he saw the graffiti sprayed on the construction site billboard. In bright-red letters the words were: NO MORE YUPPIES, and another, YUPPIES SUCK!

The smile was still on Smalls' face as he plodded barefoot to the kitchen. He turned up the volume so he could hear the president of the company who was building the condos but first the footage switched to any angry resident. "Change makes people mad," the elderly, white woman said. "I've been living here since the 70s and now I'm being forced out."

It then dawned on Smalls so he snapped to attention. "That's exactly what happened to Roscoe in First Ward." He spoke aloud to no one in particular.

A middle-aged, white man now spoke to the cameras. "This was a neighborhood of artists and blue-collar workers, but now with the Yuppies moving in, the high property taxes are going to push all the native residents out and then all the traditions of Elizabeth will be destroyed by people who won't give a hoot about our history and memories."

"And how does that make you feel?"

"Almost mad enough to kill," the man answered honestly.

Smalls appreciated the man's honesty. Now, it all made sense. What he now understood was that Roscoe wanted to kill all the white people in First Ward because they were intruders, invading against the sanctity of his memories. Suddenly, this wasn't so difficult to understand because now it was precisely what the little, old man wanted to do.

He activated his beeper. He got more news, and he lost his appetite. There was another set of murders in First Ward and Puff didn't do them. What did this mean? Smalls knew that it meant that Roscoe had come out of the closet with a vengeance.

The patrol car went fast.

"In here, sir," a cop motioned from the doorway where he indicated the chalk marks on the floor. "Mama Bear. Papa Bear. Baby Bear."

"Only three?" Smalls inquired flatly.

"Yes sir, that's all there were. Family members, real quiet people." He started to walk away. "The weapons, well sir, he didn't try to bury the weapons. He apparently put some thought into the act, placing them in a manner that forensics think is symbolic." He motioned with his head. "This way, sir." He pointed. "If you're willing to believe such a thing, it looks like the guns are kissing."

Smalls looked off. This was a clue, all right, but he pried for more info. "Anything else? Something more literal. While everyone seemed so enchanted by the so-called symbolism of smooching pistols, did anyone exercise the good sense to check out the ballistics?"

"The bullets that killed the Parton family were all fired from the weapons we discovered."

"The ones kissing?"

"Yes sir."

Smalls departed, but he hadn't even driven around the block before he knew what he had to do. Instantly, he started to feel trapped, but still he had to do it. He would bring Roscoe in for questioning, and if possible, lock his ass up forever, but first he had to decipher the secret of the kissing guns.

BANG!

The car couldn't move fast enough to get him across town. If he was going to make a case against Roscoe, the journey would start at one of the most unlikeliness places in town, City Hall.

After conferring with the clerk, the man left, returning with a stack of dusty folders. "The Wards," he intoned. "There were four of them and they were all surveyed by a civil engineer by the name of Charles Mahon. It says the boundaries of the wards are shown on the city's 1875 centennial map." Hold on, and let me see if I can't locate one of those suckers.' He shuffled noisily through some papers in a tan file cabinet. "Here we are," he happily exclaimed." "There's First Ward right there and, yes, the boundaries does include all the streets you mentioned. Now, as for the property deeds, I'll have to check back through the old realtor's log, and boy, that could take forever. Hell, since you're the law, come on back and do it yourself."

It was almost three hours later when Smalls left the County's Office of Deeds and Registrars, but he did have the info he desired. He had successfully discovered the name of the black family that had lived in the house where the Parton family had recently been brutally terminated, and he was certain the connection would yield him answers.

From roughly the same time as Roscoe's family had resided on Sixth Street, The Hoskins family had lived on Seventh Street in a huge grey house where the Parton townhouse now stood, and if he was right about the implications of his "smooching guns" theory, then Roscoe, as a child, had kissed someone in the Hoskins' household. At once, he eliminated all the males, and of the three females he was left with, he zeroed in on the one who was born around the same time as Roscoe. *Wilhemenia!*

It took him another two and a half hours before he was able to flush Wilhemenia out. She had gotten lost in the paperwork after graduating from high school and working as a part-time librarian. She had briefly married and the name change had left him stranded to his elbows in a paper trail that ended in divorce court. In 1990, he picked up her trail again and after following her through a maddening series of apartment changing, he had her exact location pinpointed.

Her 'paper' biography had her tagged as an intelligent, industrious, independent woman, and from all accounts, she had known Roscoe. They had lived a block away from each other, had attended the same church, and had gone to the same neighborhood school-----but had they kissed? He would soon find out.

After about thirty minutes, Smalls' tailbone started to ache, and he wanted to abandon the stakeout just to get out of the car to stretch his legs. Ten minutes after this, his tailbone still ached, but, in addition, he now had to piss. Now, he truly considered aborting his stakeout of the Merriman Avenue home, but it was then, at that moment, that his luck changed.

It was her!

Wilhemenia loaded her arms with grocery bags and headed up the sidewalk to the house. Smalls impulsively chewed on the concept of helping her carry in the bags, but ruled it out. Watching impassively, he gathered that she didn't live alone, or she ate like a water buffalo. *That was a lot of food.* He gave her almost enough time to put away the groceries before he rang the doorbell. Smalls got his credentials ready.

"I'm Police Chief Smalls and I would like to come in to ask you a few simple questions about someone I think you may know."

She allowed Smalls in. "I don't want to answer any questions that may get someone in trouble," she said firmly.

"Please, relax," Smalls said softly. "I'm not here to put any of your friends in jail. I just need to know about something that may or may not have happened to you a long time ago."

"*Too me?!*" The voice was higher than normal. "I have never been the victim of a crime."

"Let's see, then. Your name is-----"

"You've already gotten that right. At the door, remember?"

"Okay, as a little girl, you lived in First Ward, didn't you? On Seventh Street."

"Lived on Seventh Street when it was Earle Village too. Seems like I spent most of my life on Seventh Street."

"You attended Alexander-------."

"Yes. Alexander was just for grades one through three. Then we went to First Ward to complete the fourth, fifth, and sixth grades. "

Smalls fidgeted. "I want to ask you about something, a little incident that might have made you feel real good as a girl."

"Like what?"

"Your very first kiss, perhaps."

"*My first kiss!?* Wilhemenia exclaimed hotly, her face in a frown. "May I see your badge again?"

Smalls laid the badge on the table. "It's real, I assure you."

Wilhemenia scribbled down the badge number. "Now, if this is someone's idea of a joke, and you're not who you say you are, then you should leave right now." She pointed towards the door.

Smalls sighed. "I am exactly who I say I am, and I am here on official police business. I sincerely apologize-----"

"Just ask your questions."

"Do you know or remember Roscoe Brown?"

"I remember Roscoe, haven't seen him in over twenty years."

"You and ol' Roscoe were pretty close way back then, weren't you?"

"And just what in the hell is that supposed to mean?"

Smalls didn't back down. "Didn't the two of you play Mommy and Daddy together?"

Her eyebrows shot up, and her mouth flew open. "I beg your pardon. No, we did not."

"You-you kissed him."

"*Kissed him?* You're out of your mind, and I'm telling you to leave. *Now.*"

Smalls stood. "Are you denying that you and Roscoe were lovers?"

"We were children. That hardly qualifies us a lovers."

"But you did kiss?"

"How in the hell you know what we did?"

Smalls stepped closer, threatening. "I don't know, but you are going to tell me." He winked slyly. "Obstructing justice may not be a term that pops up in your everyday conversation," he sneered, but it's kinda like a STD. You know, something you just don't want to catch." He backed away. "You and Roscoe Brown never kissed when you were young?"

"No"

"And you're sure?'

"I should know who I kissed, shouldn't I?'

"Well, I think you're lying."

"Why would I do something like that?"

"Who else was Roscoe sweet on in your house? Maybe he was two-timing you and sneaking off in the dark, kissing one of your sisters."

"This is crazy," the woman surmised. "And why is so important to the police who Roscoe was kissing when he was too young to know what he was doing. You act like kissing is a crime."

"It matters."

"Is Roscoe in trouble?"

"Would you try to protect him if he was in trouble?"

"Depends."

"What about if I told you that Roscoe may be responsible for some very terrible crimes, and that this whole city could be affected by what he's done and is still doing. Is that the kind of individual you would want to protect? The man is a monster. Roscoe Brown is a terrible,

terrible monster and I need all the help I can get in putting him away so he can't hurt any more people." Smalls reached for the woman's hand. "Please."

"Okay, what can I do?"

" Thank you, thank you a lot. Now, this is what I need for you to do, if you will. I need for you to go with me tomorrow morning, back over to where you used to live on Seventh Street, and we'll just take a walk around. I want to test your memory a little bit. Can you make this happen?"

"I work in the morning."

"We could met on your way to work as long as it's daylight. I promise you won't be late for work."

Wilhemenia Hoskins smiled glumly. That must have been some kiss. I'll see you tomorrow at eight o'clock."

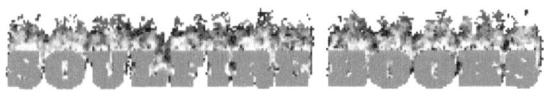

Tuesday morning, December 30th, was leaning towards sunshine, but at 8:00, the sun was hiding behind an overcast cloud, exposing herself naughtily, being suggestive. Smalls was joined in the parking lot of the Afro-American Cultural Center by Wilhemenia at 8:03, and they drove up to the Parton townhouse. They began their tour at the front with Wilhemenia describing the way things were when she lived there as a little girl.

"Down the street on the next corner was a pool room and across from that was The Chicken Shack. Tutterow's Grocery was next to that. A lot of people would come this way, right beside our house to get to those places on Seventh Street."

"What about out back?"

"This is where our back door would have been. Over there was what everyone called "The Alley". There were only about six houses on the whole street."

Smalls said nothing, moving her closer to the spot where the guns had been found. He wanted to know what had been there, but he wanted her to tell him.

"And right here," Wilhemenia smiled, remembering, "is where all the girls played hopscotch."

Smalls spoke gently, not wanting to break her trance as she traveled back in her mind. "Why don't you name some of the girls who used to play back here? Do you remember any of their names?"

"Yes, I remember." Wilhemenia's voice sounded dreamy, distant. "My sisters, of course. Then there were Roscoe's own sisters, BeBe, Sheila, Pookie, sometimes Charlotte and….." She paused.

"And what was here?" Smalls asked quietly, nudging her closer.

"There was a fence right here, well, not a real fence, more like chicken wire or something. That's where the big boys played basketball."

Did Roscoe play?"

"No, he was too little." She looked away. "Over there, a guy named Arthur Griffin stayed. "He's head of the school board now. A narrow dirt road separated his house from where we now stand." She pointed. "Butch Blackmon and his family lived across the street."

Smalls had her in position now. "Did anything used to be here?" He held his breath; waiting.

Wilhemenia stared, looking around as if measuring the distance from where they stood with the long-erased place where she had played hopscotch as a little girl, and for a very long time, she was quiet, uncertain. Then. A twinkle in her eyes, followed with a smile. *Something remembered.*

Smalls dared not rush her so he waited, still and silent.

"Used to be a damn tree right here and you're right," she smiled. "I remember it now. Roscoe did kiss me, right under the shade tree."

Smalls felt James Brown good. The symbolism of the kissing guns had just been solved.

By 11:55, the last unit of the offensive moved silently into place, and from the designated rendezvous point churned menacingly onto Corona Street in Dalton Village. The early morning attack was designed specifically for the apprehension of the human. The cat was not to be engaged or provoked, and everyone hoped that Roscoe could be persuaded to come along without incident. After all, they merely wanted to question him. No big deal if everything was handled smoothly. However, Puff would be under surveillance at all times. They wanted to study the cat's every move, to see and to learn what it would do in Roscoe's absence. They also wanted to probe for any weaknesses

the cat might have before they decided whether to risk capturing it or simply killing it.

Then, suddenly, they converged on Apartment A, and in a matter of seconds, it was contained, surrounded, sealed off and everyone was in position.

"Let's pray he comes along peacefully." Smalls rapped loudly on the door, but there was no response. He knocked again and searched for the doorbell. He found none. He knocked louder.

"Allow me," Berkowitz demanded. He pounded upon the door even more loudly.

The lights popped on in Apartment B, and a tired lady stuck her head out of the front door. "He moved," she said sleepily. "Been gone about a week."

"You're sure?"

"If you don't believe me, kick the door down and find out for yourself," She slammed the door to her apartment.

"Kick the door down," Berkowitz ordered.

CHAPTER ELEVEN

New Year's Day 1998

Sipping from a cocktail, Smalls began the long-delayed search of his soul, and for the first time in over thirty years didn't find it necessary to field test his conscience because whatever he decided to do, he would do.

For a long time, he simply sat, with his legs crossed, staring out of the bay windows, gazing at the clouds. Since he had no real tradition or experience with outright honesty, and since this was his first occasion, he didn't know what to expect. Yet after a brief second, he confessed that all he felt at the moment was a silent lucidity.

Gripped by the terrible enormity of what was about to happen, he spit upon the ridiculous notion that the Army could be reasoned with. Therefore, the incessant need to worry. After all, the Army was no paper tiger, and would eagerly immerse his face in a toilet bowl soiled with shit. The feeling, he clearly understood, wasn't preposterous. The US Army was not to be fucked with.

By mid-morning, he thought he had dispelled enough of his doubt and reservations to make the necessary phone call, but he hadn't. Even at such a critical juncture in his life, he was still not above being selfish, thinking only of himself and his own personal welfare. Hell, this was the Army he would be taunting with his disobedience, and for this deliberate disrespect, they would go to extreme length to punish him. He knew this, so the fear was justified.

He turned away from the phone.

Within a few hours, the McCall woman would die. Then her husband. And the killings would not stop if he couldn't reverse the Order. He tried to spur himself into action by settings his jaw tight, steeling his eyes, and hardening his heart, but he failed to pass muster

He moved further away from the phone. The damned thing disturbed him, and he was in no need to be chastised by his apparent cowardice. But when he thought hard enough about it, the one logical conclusion to be reached was that he didn't owe the McCalls shit. Or Charlotte.

He wasn't amused at any by of this so he hoped that Berkowitz was a man of his word.

He picked up the phone and his hands silently sweated, the gooey perspiration dropping from his outstretched fingers as he dialed the number.

The die was cast.

Meg rushed down the concourse, almost frantic, nearly running. She slowed momentarily, following a bunch of slow-moving tourists. At the gift shoppe, she turned reflexively and peeked through the glass window into the terminal. She gasped. It was the same two men. Both tall and dressed in trench coats. One of them glared at her, then looked away quickly. She took a step back behind a column. She peeked once more. The men were conferring softly, whispering into each other's ear, looking in her direction. It was them!

She rushed towards the ladies bathroom. Surely, they would not follow her there. She paused at the door haltingly, glancing over her shoulder before barging on down the stairs. She skipped steps, moving fast. Three-quarters down the steps she looked over to her left and noticed one of the men riding the escalator, He was going down. He stared at her. He nodded.

On the bottom, a hefty man moved in front of the stairs. She gasped in panic. He was waiting for her and instinctively she turned, intending to run back the way she had come. She pushed her way through the throng of people on the staircase and as she neared the top, she saw first the shoes, then the dun-colored hem of the coat. Then she saw the man. He reached out to her roughly, pulling her onto the landing.

"Don't panic," he said. "We're friends."

Slowly, but deliberately he pushed Meg back onto the steps, nudging her down towards the ground level. He spoke something lowly into a device hidden under the lapel of his coat. "Everything's fine," he said to Meg.

At the bottom, they were met by two other men. The hefty man squinted at her and pulled her alongside the wall next to a Rent-A-Car booth. For a moment, he was quiet, watching the other two men, who turned this way and that, scanning in all directions; looking. When the hefty man elected to speak, his voice was controlled and filled with authority. "Your life is in danger as well as your husband and daughter, and we have been assigned to protect you."

"By who? Why?"

"Our job is to protect you, not answer questions." The hefty man stood erect. He stared her directly in her eyes, and it was a dare not to speak. He, then, pulled her down into a recess into an interior wall. Moving her away from the rope-offed, red-carpeted ticket counter as his two companions disappeared into the crowd, it was evident to Meg that she---they---could not leave yet.

In desperation, Meg attempted to move away from the man. Swiftly, he grabbed her shoulder. "What do you think you are doing?" he whispered coldly.

"Are you the police?"

"No, but I have my orders. Mrs. McCall." The hefty man stepped closer, whispering. "You were told by your husband to come immediately to the airport, is that correct?"

"Yes, but I was told to meet a woman in jeans, a sweater-----."

"And bright, red lipstick" he added.

"Hello," said an attractive woman in Guess jeans, a white sweater, and the brightest red lipstick Meg had ever seen. "My name is Ona."

She roughly pushed Meg out into the aisle. "Let's move it, Toots. Head for the nearest exit."

"Where am I going? Where are you taking me?"

"Move it!"

"I'll scream," Meg warned. "Where are you taking me?"

"Screaming will only show what little regards you have for your life as well as your husband and daughter. We are here to help."

Meg's body stiffened, defiance blazing in her eyes. "And what if I don't believe you?"

The hefty man's stone gaze grew less impassive, but his cold eyes did not change. "We cannot force her. Our orders are merely to accompany her to safety, If she resists, then it is of no further concern of ours. The offer of protection was made, and I will personally notify General Berkowitz of her refusal."

One of the men turned quickly, sensing danger. He apologized to Meg and then knocked her unconscious. "Let's go," he uttered, gathering Meg in his arms as if she was a toddler.

They pushed through the door to the waiting car.

Meg was alert, but still groggy when the car pulled up beside the entrance of a posh hotel on the fringes of the city. The moon was a pale, neon orb sparkling over the roof of the hotel's service exit.

"Don't try to talk," Meg was cautioned. "Listen. Your life is threatened by people you cannot defend yourself against. They will go to extraordinary lengths to execute their orders, and they are very resourceful."

Meg gulped down a throatful of air.

"This is who you are for the time being." Meg was handed a driver's license. "You will be made to resemble the photo, Mrs. McCall. That will be the most we can do for you. You must do the rest."

"Like what?"

"Forget about being Megan McCall. You must immediately become someone else, and you must act the part. Give me the ring."

"Huh?'

"The wedding ring. Give it to me. The fancy necklace, too. Think plain Jane, Mrs. McCall. Now, walk into the hotel. Don't look at anyone directly and cross the lobby to the elevator. Your room is 426. Don't stop. Go directly there and lock yourself in. Do you understand, Mrs. McCall?"

Meg nodded slowly.

"Shortly after you get to your room, someone---a woman—will come to re-arrange your look, if you will. You will be Libby Quentin. Don't open your door for anyone besides the woman who identifies herself as Brittany, your daughter's name which should make it easy to remember." The hefty man paused for effect. "Don't use the phone, not even to order room service. I will personally have your meal sent up to you."

"I-I don't think I can eat," Meg complained. "I just want this over with."

"Now, go."

Out of the car, Meg was suddenly aware of how cold it was and hugging herself to ward off the stinging chill, she scurried across the empty parking lot into the foyer of the hotel. Upon her hurried entrance, a bustling gust of wind swept across the lobby, ruffling the pages of an elderly gentleman's newspaper. He stopped reading and began to watch her, his keen eyes glued to her every movement. Their eyes met over the crumpled top of the newspaper. She looked away. He didn't. He placed the paper in his lap, and reached into his coat pocket. *Cigarettes.* Then he abruptly headed for the elevators.

Startled, Meg quickly surveyed the thinning, boisterous crowd as people moved from the hotel's bar and restaurant to various other destinations, but the man remained close at her elbow. She deftly pressed UP and smiled at the elderly gentleman while keeping a careful eye on the elevator's downward plunge where she waited for it.

The man removed his glasses and gently stuffed them into his jacket and Meg secretly noticed how strong his hands looked. The elevator stopped on 4, and Meg fidgeted slightly. The elevator began moving again. The man tugged nervously at the sleeves of his jacket as he watched her in the polished glow of the mirrored elevator paneling.

The elevator was now on the third floor, then the arrow darkened, jumping to two, lighting it up in a florescent green triangle. After a moment, the elevator was on the go again.

"I must have a newspaper," Meg announced, a split second before the elevator's door hissed open.

"Take mine," the man offered politely."

"Thanks," Meg said, "but I couldn't do that." Moving away quickly, the elevator doors snapped closed behind her.

She stood under a small archway where a newspaper rack was pushed into a tiny niche next to a stamp machine. She dangled a handful of coins and then hurriedly stuffed them into the slot, exchanging the money for a copy of the USA TODAY, but sudden movement to her left caused her involuntary alarm. She couldn't be sure, but the woman speaking to the Oriental man was pointing at her. The man appeared to thank the woman and then moved towards her, his approach swift.

They traded worried glances, Meg stumbling to the side at an angle to the unsmiling man's path. He neared, but at the last second turned into a door she had not paid any attention to as he disappeared into the gym.

It was impossible for her not to breathe hard, her lips parted to expel air that reeked of fear. She had to get to her room. She caught the elevator with two old ladies and UP they zoomed.

On the fourth floor, the elevator opened up opposite a huge Romare Bearden collage that hung above a pair of rubber plants and a copper-colored spittoon. Gold-plated arrows indicated that rooms 417-427 veered to the left of the ice machine. The odd-numbered rooms were to her right so she crossed over, clutching the electronic key tightly in her fist. The final room on the right was her. 426.

She eagerly let herself in and even before the door had quietly closed behind her, she had the lights ON and she snapped ON the TV on her way to the heating unit. There, she twisted the oblong knob to ten and with only a slight delay, the heat whoosed into action.

Drawing back from the window, she flopped down heavily on the comfortable bed and channel-surfed as images quickly flickered back and forth at her. She stopped briefly when she recognized Steve

McQueen in Papillon. She vaguely recalled the movie, having had to read the book as part of her freshman college English class, but after five minutes switched stations, moving aimlessly through the channels distracting herself with the eerie blur.

There was a rap at the door. Then another. Meg grew tense and silent. *Another knock.* She tip-toed to the door and through the peephole caught the distorted vision of a woman. Then came a series of knocks, these more insistent than any of the ones that preceded them.

"Who's there?"

"It's me. Brittany."

The woman with the adopted name entered the room. She was tall and athletic, as graceful as a ballerina. She had a long, elegant neck and her pale, delicate features hinted of a stuffy aristocracy although she was dressed demurely.

There were no formalities to be dispensed with so Brittany was reassuringly professional. "I have the needed things," she said brusquely. "Where's the photo?" She was already out of her coat, rummaging through the bag, rattling cans and boxes. "The photo?" she asked again.

Brittany's head swung erratically from the photo to Meg's face and back again, and a frown started at the curve of the woman's lip as if she did not welcome the task ahead. She took a short breath and ran her fingers gently through Meg's hair, examining the texture and studying the color. She stood behind Meg, looking into the mirror as she piled Meg's hair on the top of her head and then let it cascade softly back around her shoulders.

"Sit," she ordered.

From the bag, the woman extracted a rumpled, green smock that she fitted over Meg's head like a soft canopy, covering her upper body. Then she was busy removing items from the bag. Hair coloring. Scissors. A razor.

"Now, I need you to turn away from the mirror," the woman demanded flatly. "It makes me nervous for my clients to watch me as I work." She touched Meg's shoulder lightly. "Don't get me wrong, I'm good at this but I'm more comfortable when no one's peeking, so please indulge me, okay?" She sprayed Meg's hair and gently picked up the razor. "Thanks so much. Now, what questions do you want me to try to answer?"

"What is this a------?'

The words stopped in Meg's throat. At first, the pressure was a warm, wet prick on her neck, but with a slight turn of her head, the pain became more direct, more red-hot. She tried to shift her head to pull her neck away from the scorching, searing penetration, but she couldn't. It was as if something had snapped open in her throat, burning a red-hot liquid fire across her neck and she couldn't scream; couldn't gasp. Then just as abruptly, the fire became ice cold as rich, red blood seeped silently out of the thin incision the razor had made from one of her ears to the other.

Meg's eyes strayed down upon the blood, then they opened in fright and astonishment, then they clamped shut in utter disbelief. A second later, she was dead.

Smalls hung up the phone slowly and held his head mournfully in his hands. They had killed her. Now, without even remorse or pity, they were probably on their way to kill him.......McCall.....Berkowitz, and from all indications, each of them could stay alive for only as long as they could stay hidden. Hiding and running comprised the total spectrum of their options. It wasn't a rosy picture.

The two men waited for Smalls to speak and they feared the worst. "I'm sorry, McCall," he whispered, "but they found Meg dead in a hotel room."

"*What!?*" McCall shouted. "*No!*" he whispered. "It can't be. There is some mistake, there has to be. It-it can't be. No."

"That call," Smalls intoned to Berkowitz, "was from the police chief in Seattle. He was informed to contact me in the event of something." He stared sadly at McCall, "well....."

McCall sobbed bitterly. He went limp, his body propelled downward until his head was between his legs where he retched and gasped for air. He cried out pitifully, his mind reeling. His mouth dry. He tried to stand, to come to grips with what he had heard and to focus, but he was unable to. In an attempt to steady himself, he massaged his temples, trying to restore the blood back to his face. Everything seemed dim; darkening. His pulse still raced while his body temperature seemed to plunge, plummeting into a region where his basal metabolism was suspended and all body heat cancelled.

McCall fainted!

"Get him over to the bed," Smalls shrieked. "Loosen his collar, let him get some air. Oh my God!" the police chief shrieked, momentarily losing his composure. He stared at General Berkowitz. "They're here, aren't they?"

General Berkowitz nodded. "Or on the way."

"What do we do?"

"Get to Washington. There, I have friends, contacts. We'll be safe there." He glanced at McCall. "God, I feel awful about his wife, but we better get him up. We're going to have to hurry and be ready to leave as soon as I make a phone call or two."

The General stepped into the cozy den and sat by the phone close to the bar next to the faux fireplace. He was somewhat agitated as he dug into his wallet for the private, personal number of the one person he knew he could absolutely trust under the circumstances: George Leonard from The Joint Chiefs of Staff.

Two things Berkowitz knew he had in his favor. One, a professional courtesy owed him by Leonard, and even more important, Leonard detested Sherman. In theory, this should prove to be a safe rite of passage.

General Berkowitz congratulated himself. Yeah, Leonard was the ticket, and it was at this precise moment that he realized he had an engraved invitation to the party, and all his current fears collapsed, reforming themselves into tiny magnets of hope and optimism.

He made the phone call.

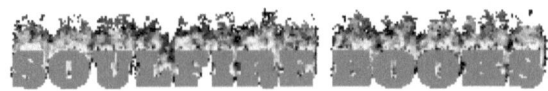

George Leonard sat in the study of his upstate New York penthouse, overlooking snow-capped mountain peaks to the west. He twisted the cord on the phone round and round, entwining the soft, pliant rubber between his fingers. The movement, the absent coiling was done without reason, was simply a distraction for his hands----and mind. There was not sufficient time to think through the ABCs of his choice, but the oppressive question of what he would do could not be left open. Too much, on both sides, hung in the balance, and all that really was required was as primitive as a grunt.

Either yes. Or maybe no.

Neither response would disrupt his sleep. He just didn't care to be infected by the petty trivia that would accompany and pursue the warmth or chill of his verdict. Leonard's smile spilled out of the sides of his mouth brightly. He felt mythical, He didn't just reach or make decisions. That was too weak, much too frail. Instead, what he did was to render verdicts! A simple nod of his head could mean sustenance and security whereas, a frown.....well, that would be a bitter pill to swallow.

George Leonard delighted in his patented search for the ulterior motive behind every deed or action because these, he knew, were the discount prices that men paid for their triumphs. Nothing infuriated or disturbed him as long as he was allowed to anticipate or to manage the degree of manipulation involved.

He was a stickler for well-devised fraud, and no one was more knowledgeable than he at how to choose sides in lethal, cloak-and-dagger politics. He was also highly talented and extremely well-versed in the art of divvying up the spoils of war no matter who thought they had won.

George Leonard simply knew what he knew. He did not consider himself an enigma. Actually, he considered himself the spiritual heir of whomever had said "*Every man for himself.*"

"Sherman," he spoke into the receiver of the phone.

"Yes, my friend."

"I just received the oddest phone call."

"He did make contact?"

"Just as you predicted, but I caution you that he enlightened me a good deal more than you did. Frankly, he was rather eloquent in his appeal."

"And why shouldn't he be, my friend. The guilty can plead his case like no other."

"But isn't what you propose a bit much?" He paused, toying with Sherman, flirting with the man's impatience. "Look, I'm not expecting you to compromise your little scheme, old boy, so don't frighten yourself out of your wits. I'm going to help you grab the son-of-a-bitch by his nuts, but I will have you know that it was no easy feat, this, my decision to assist you."

"I understand human nature, my friend."

"Great. Your bird is at this address. I took the liberty of tracing the number myself. Dispatch your goons swiftly because he awaits my callback in forty-five minutes. Good day, my friend, you'll be hearing from me when the need arises.

The congested ache inside McCall's head was like a piercing dagger thrust, tearing at his eyes as he squinted hopefully, desiring to shut OFF the pain, but he still was unable to focus. He stood up, pacing back and forth beside the bed, between the chair. Everything remained fuzzy, abstract, and to his bewilderment, he felt abnormal, grudgingly accepting his wife's horrible death.

He stopped pacing and stood quietly at the mirror on a dresser. He pensively acknowledged his haggard appearance and wondered----- *what's next*, but after a few self-absorbed moments of this inspection, he faced Smalls and Berkowitz. "I must go for a walk."

"Don't get lost, McCall," Berkowitz howled, 'because as soon as I hear back from my contact, we must be ready to leave at once." He glared at his watch. "We're expecting you back in fifteen minutes.

Smalls opened the door, stared out into the beyond of the darkness, then closed the door. "I can't go with you," he mumbled. "I have to go. My first priority is to go get Mag and make the necessary arrangements for......you know. That is my priority."

"Listen, McCall, be sensible. Your wife's body will be released to her family and as harsh as this may sound, you can't attend the funeral."

"What!" McCall exploded. "Surely, you're mad. The woman was my wife and if you think for one second that I'm not going to be there with her, then both of you are crazy. I'll go with you to Washington, and I'll even allow her family to make the arrangements, but, get this gentlemen, "I'm going to my wife's funeral."

Several minutes later, a dark-colored sedan came down the street, driving past McCall slowly. The occupants of the car eyed McCall suspiciously, but McCall never noticed as he merely continued his stroll down the block. Rounding the curb seconds later, a brown van with wood panels approached. It slowed down, revealing at least two men inside. It inched forward after getting a close look at McCall.

Sixty seconds later, McCall spun around and headed back. They would be expecting him. Under a streetlamp, his shadow revolved around the crushed shell of an orange juice can, and upon reaching the next corner, the night was violated by noise.

Gunshots!

McCall froze, stiffening, wanting confirmation. This time it was definite. Gunfire!

"On my God!" McCall groaned as he saw three men erupt from the front door of Smalls' house and jump into the waiting, brown van. At almost the same time, the dark sedan careened around the corner behind him.

"That's him!" he heard someone shout and in response a bullet whizzed just below his ear.

McCall turned quickly, mystified, but lucid enough to run. He dove behind a clump of shrubs and a garbage can as another bullet zinged off the pavement near his feet. Men shouted at one another as car doors slammed. McCall dazedly picked himself up and ran rapidly between two houses, jack-knifing over a waist-high fence at the lower section of a three-car garage. He scrambled through some bushes, tripped, scraping and cutting his elbow, but the men were approaching the fence, yelling orders so he ran furiously, feeling the desperate heat of pursuit.

At the bottom of the hill, there were other houses. He ran past them, not slowing down, not daring to cast a glance over his shoulder. He didn't know where he was, but he knew he had to get away, far away from whatever had happened at Chief Smalls house, and the men who had done it.

Gasping for air, the only sounds he heard were the ragged melody of his own breathing. Maybe the men had given up. Maybe they had called OFF the search. Maybe they had gone back to their cars and had left.

He slowed down, stopped, lay prone. He had to rest, to think. Sweat covered him, but he ignored the stickiness of his clothes. He began to breathe deeply, inhaling large lungfuls of the cold, stinging air. His nostrils flared wildly at the sharp intake of oxygen, then deflated gradually.

Two minutes passed.

Then three.

McCall climbed to his feet, the numbing sense of despair reduced but not altogether gone. He had to make it back to the streets, to Smalls' house. Yes, they would never look for him to go back there and surely, they would not hang around the scene of the crime. They had to be smarter than that.

He walked towards his destination and within minutes, the house came into view. Stumbling up on the porch, he opened the front door, stepping uneasily into the living room, and after what seemed a condensed eternity, he gingerly closed the door. From where he now stood, the quiet belied any tell-tale evidence of a murder. Everything was touched with a silent calm, suffused throughout with a maddening peace, but beyond the foyer was the gutter of death, where it had happened, where he knew the dead bodies were.

He had to see.

He limped across the living room floor, his knees repeatedly buckling, warping his body into an awkward, grotesque loop. At the den's entrance, he paused, his lips puckered as though he was about to whistle. Instead, he sucked in a small bit of air and peeked. He saw Smalls' body first, knotted on the floor, locked into the fetal position, his upper body a red pockmark of bullet holes. McCall gasped, moving closer. Smalls' face was almost expressionless; one eyes opened, the other, missing. A bullet had torn it out of its socket, and the morbid orb lay mired in drying blood. Saliva had poured from his lips, congealing there, tubular gobs still clinging to his chin.

McCall crept away, shuffling towards the sofa, peeking behind it. He already knew what to expect, what he would find. The General's body was sprawled on the floor like a toppled plastic mannequin, arms askew, legs splayed widely. *Dead.* His face was already a cement grey, plastered opaquely with the abstract imprint of death. His countenance, unlike Smalls, was visibly expressive, poignant in its abject terror.

Suddenly, McCall heard movement. He turned.

"Mr. McCall, I presume."

Everything, at once, slowed down, and into this turbulent impasse, McCall's life flashed swiftly before his eyes. He had lost. The three gunshots erased McCall out of existence, and into the need for a eulogy.

Ashes to ashes.

CHAPTER TWELVE

S herman sat with two other men at a conference table. The room was dark. The phone disconnected. Apparently, the men did not desire to be interrupted.

Sherman quickly assessed the situation, cashing in on the fact that he could now count on the influence of Georg e Leonard in the event the predicament turned dicey or simply needed a nudge to get it unstuck. At any rate, he sensed he would leave this little meeting with a big send-off for his Charlotte Protocol. He drew his face into a tight mask, scrutinizing the men carefully. They had given him such a chilly reception yesterday, but, at least, he had not been cut adrift to shoulder the project alone, and this was reason enough for him to feel optimistic. No, well, opportunistic, might be a better word, but he smiled confidently just the same.

Tired of examining the other men, part of the Army's Technical Bio-chemical Division, Sherman focused on himself. Though he was almost retirement age, he was still more than mildly obsessed with upward mobility into the higher echelon of the military ruling elite.

Hence the need for The Charlotte Protocol. His eyes widened. He knew that behind his back, many deprecated his ideas and whispered that he was insane, but they were the fools. All of them. *Imbeciles!* They were all busboys and maître d's stuffed inside the wrong uniforms, strutting around in their fancy military gear when they were better-suited to parking cars or waiting tables.

Sherman had to check his enthusiasm. He was starting to tingle all over and he didn't want to appear fanatical as some ignoramus had termed it. He, then, fixed the men with a hard, cold glare. "If I say there is no time, then that is exactly what I mean. If there was time, I'd be out either sipping hot tea or guzzling cold beer, and not holed up with a pair of jackasses here in Salt Lake City."

"Actually, sir, we're sixty miles west of there."

"Who gives a damn, it's still Utah, and if I don't get the shit I need, then Charlotte is going to turn into a catastrophe."

"Like Winkler, sir?"

At the mention of Winkler, Sherman's boiling anger blossomed, seemingly ready to explode, but suddenly he gained mastery of his temper and lapsed into more controlled babbling. "Is it possible that I have been misunderstood. The whole country hangs in the balance, and dammit, trust me, this is no illusion on my part, and I'm clearly in total control of my mental faculties, so dammit, don't think otherwise regardless of what you may hear whispered." He lowered his voice slightly. "The country, as we know it, gentlemen, is in grave jeopardy, and I'm concerned."

"And the little biological experiment you wish to execute in Charlotte is supposed to prove......what?"

"They're already here," Sherman spat. "Dammit, they're here."

"Who, aliens?"

"No, the frigging cat, you moron. Don't you get it?"

"You think we don't know of you, sir," one of the men sneered. "Well, your reputation precedes you. You are a murderer of innocent men, women, and children; the Mad Assassin of Winkler. Now, you want to encore in Charlotte. Personally, I think you quite mad." He shook his head sadly. "And we're not going to allow you to slaughter innocent people in Charlotte."

"And you?" Smalls fixed his gaze on the other man.

"Frankly, I think you're off your rocker." He glared at Sherman. "Who do you think you're fooling? You, somehow, believe this has something to do with Winkler, don't you, and you're using all your considerable influence to convince everyone on The Hill that it does." The man studied Sherman's face for either acknowledgment or denial, but recognized neither. "According to all reports, Winkler collapsed before you had the chance to use it to your advantage and you're still upset, and now you see Charlotte as a second opportunity, another chance to redeem your Star Wars Project, and to beg The Pentagon for the billions needed to complete work on your chemical laser". The man nodded to himself. "That's it, isn't it? You never gave up and now this strange, yellow cat has come along to provide all the justification you need to cry wolf again." The man grunted accusingly. "You want to make others think that Charlotte is another Winkler." He pointed at his colleague. "I'm with him, I won't allow you to kill innocent people in Charlotte."

Sherman stormed from the conference. "Just try stopping me."

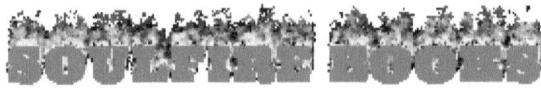

It had rained every day Sherman had been in Charlotte, and the same thing had been forecast for tomorrow. *Rain!* What a way to celebrate Friday, but, despite the gloom, he was out enjoying his meal. Tomorrow wasn't going anywhere.

He was wildly surprised at the excellent service at The Campania. The restaurant was shimmering with its lovely golden walls, rich wood, and candle-light. A perfect foil to the drizzle outside.

Sherman found the lamb osso buco quite elegant and succulent. Superb. He dined quietly, absorbed in the silent melancholy of his thoughts. So, this was Charlotte.

He asked himself a few choice questions, and his basic contempt for the city grew even more swollen because somewhere in this candy-coated metropolis rested the final equation of his great puzzle: *the mystery of that damned cat!*

His calculations had to be right, they had to be. Puff was Winkler. The very thought left a bitter taste in his mouth, so he quickly stabbed his fork into the strawberry cheesecake and devoured it in two short bites. He had always taken enormous pride in knowing that he could always count of himself to get things right, so it occurred to him that the papers retrieved from Smalls' home had simply misinterpreted the facts. After all, Smalls had known nothing of Winkler. If so, he would have, at once, identified the similarities. He, for one, was not foolish enough to believe that Puff was some hopped-up feline spurred into action by the razing of some slum neighborhood. Puff, he knew, had nothing at all to do with such absurdity, and surely the cat had no real ties of affection to any earthling, Roscoe Brown included. Puff had nothing to do with any of the nonsense contained in Smalls' writings.

He had automatically assumed, upon reading the data in Smalls' writings that the toxins identified in the soil at the creek where the cat had been buried would match precisely the toxins found in the soil at Winkler, but no. And Sherman had found that perplexing. Something was not quite right, but the extensive testing conducted and repeated a number of times indicated no visible or traceable links. *Could he be wrong about the cat!?* Was Winkler and Charlotte separate, isolated incidents as Berkowitz had contended? *Impossible!*

Despite the dissimilar toxicity data, he still wanted the Army's Technical Escort Unit aerial crew in search of the cat within a week. It shouldn't take any longer than that to equip their laser gun with microscopic refraction sensors that could detect Puff due to the major toxins in its body. He had deduced that after prolonged exposure to the contaminated soil through burial, it was only natural that the cat had absorbed significant levels of the toxins via its skin. Voila!

In the meantime, Sherman felt that a few reconnaissance missions inside First Ward were needed to help him concentrate on the task at hand. He so desperately wished to know if this was a textbook duplicate of Winkler. That damned cat had been permitted to run wild in that community and there was no telling who it may have affected. Sherman shuddered at the thought. With the extremely high levels of contaminants in the cat's body, it is most likely that viable amounts of the toxins could have found their way into humans by the simple act of petting the damned animal. And Lord knows if the animal had scratched some poor, unsuspecting son-of-a-bitch. Well, that was just to dammit-to-hell bad, Sherman mused because he surely wasn't about to go running all over town, checking out all the recent cases of cat-scratch fever. It would be much simple to follow the Winkler Protocol and wipe them all out. He advised himself to stick with what worked. *He got the memo.*

Winkler

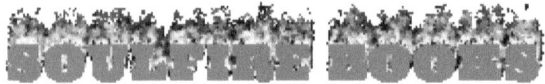

"Oh-uh."

"What's the matter?"

"Do you think we should have let those guys through? I mean, being Friday night and all. Those guys might be Army, but this is still First Ward." The CMPD officer shrugged his shoulders. "Better them than us."

The grunt and growl of the brawling thunder and the death-chamber numbness of the night reverberated through the empty streets as icy cold fear fell heavy upon the soldiers as they cruised through First Ward, cursing their predicament.

"Something is not quite right with this picture, Joe. Don't ask me what it is because I don't know, but I got a strong feeling that something is wrong."

"I wasn't going to say anything, but I'm feeling a little janky myself. Sorta like the same kind of scared I used to get at home in Texas when I used to watch horror movies." He swallowed the congestion in his throat. "Wish we had some backup."

"Me too, but we don't so let's take it slow and easy. One time through and we park somewhere where there is a lot of light."

"Weapon check, old buddy. Better safe than sorry."

A fierce blast of wind howled through the naked trees, rattling the puny branches, shaking them like empty bones. At the same time, a street light popped OFF. Seconds later, another. Then, a third."

"Christ," Joe muttered. "What the-----?"

"Flick on the high beams so we can see anything that moves in this hell-hole."

One-by-one, in sequence, the street lights popped OFF as they rode by, the darkness becoming more profane the farther they travelled inward. Their jeep rolled to a stop.

A single street light popped ON. Then another.........Another.

Every light was now ON, shining brightly up on their incandescent perches high above the streets.

"Jesus!" Elliot groaned. "Let's pull out."

One-by-one, the street lights popped OFF as they drove by.

"Something is definitely wrong here," Joe concluded, "and it smells like trouble."

"Ten-four on that, old buddy, but let's sit tight right here for a minute because I get the feeling that as long as the lights are on that we're okay."

Turning abruptly at the sound of approaching footsteps, the duo trained their weapons at the blackness which had conjured up the noise. They watched, seeing nothing until the small, stooped figure of an elderly woman shoved her way through the shadows. Both soldiers sighed in relief.

"Evening, ma'am," Joe asked politely, "you live around here?"

"Evening, boys," the old lady returned kindly.

"You live around here?" Joe repeated.

A quizzical look split the woman's face. "You'll have to speak up," she apologized. "My hearing.—"

"DO YOU LIVE AROUND HERE?"

"Oh, yes," the woman replied, "back there."

"WHERE ARE YOU GOING?"

She pointed. "To visit my grandson. My daughter lives on Brevard Street."

"GET IN. WE"LL GIVE YOU A RIDE."

The kindly, old lady hesitated, unsure. She didn't move.

"IT'S OKAY. WE'RE SOLDIERS."

The woman smiled, then climbed in, but not without difficulty, into the backseat.

"Let's get out of here," Elliot said to Joe. "This place gives me the creeps."

"Me, too. Can you imagine being out in this jungle this time of night."

"Good thing we came along because there's no telling what might have happened to her. Reminds me of my grandmother."

Joe looked back at the woman and smiled warmly. "Left or right at the corner."

She pointed.

Elliot started to say something, but instead screamed.

"What's the matter, man?" Joe croaked hoarsely.

Elliot didn't answer. He stiffened, leaning back in his seat, blood streaming down his chest.

Joe saw the tip of the blade protruding through the fabric of Elliot's uniform, the tip capped in red. He stared incomprehensively at the knife, then at the old woman, but by then she had pitched a garrote over his head and around his neck. She pulled it tight.

Joe struggled. His eyes-balls bulged out of their sockets, but the woman was tremendously strong so it was over quickly, and when the woman was certain Joe didn't have any more breaths left, she left.

The jeep smashed into a telegraph pole.

CHAPTER THIRTEEN

The New Year had just turned two weeks old. It was midnight and the man garbed in black edged silently along the front of the house, hunched down low. He filled up a dark shadow, stood still briefly, then exited. He darted out of the garish swell of the moonlight, and sank gently underneath the window, and very, very slowly inched himself up into a standing position. He peeked into the widow, and quickly moved away.

The target, Brittany McCall, had been sighted.

In a few, quick seconds, he was inside the house, but he could hear the blare of a car horn outside, a voice raised in merriment, then a slamming car door. However, inside the house, all was serene. Still, he took a deep breath to calm his nerves. This was it, and he was moving in for the kill.

His hand rose slightly, grappling with air and space, racing against time and fate until finally contact was made. Blood throbbed through his body, sprinting through collapsed veins, feeding them high doses of pure adrenaline. His palms slippery, he tried vainly to steady his hand as he twisted the knob a quarter of the way around.

The intensity of the moment was ferocious as the doorknob continued to spiral up, then around in an oval, tumbling in a circular arc to break the clasp clean, to open the door, and with a flick of his wrist, he was beside the bed of the sleeping, blonde-haired girl.

He leveled the gun.

But from out of the nothingness, the yellow cat lunged, snarling angrily. The man in black raised his arm defensively as the feline leaped, and he screamed in pain as his arm dropped to the floor, a mass of dangling nerve endings.

The cat leaped once again, but this time, it coiled its long, slinky tail around the man's neck like a lasso, and the noose grew tighter......and tighter until the man's intestines felt bloated, inflated with the noxious gases his fear had churned up. His eyes were seared by the fire of his tears as he lost control of his bowel movements.

The yellow cat gracefully mounted the man's shoulder and twisted, screwing his tail tighter. The man in black gagged hoarsely, growing weak as his eyes blinked reflexively. And when he heard the grating rasp of his next-to-last breath, he whispered aloud, "My God, forgive my sins."

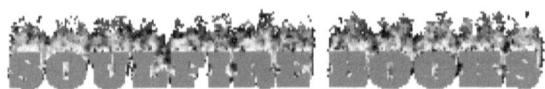

Brittany licked her upper lips and found that her mouth didn't taste so fresh. *Where was she?* She closed her hooded eyes, then re-opened them slowly, stretching them wide. Now, she felt pain. She clawed apart her blouse, searching for the source of the stinging inflammation. She pulled aside her brassiere, and peeled it away from her flesh. She gasped aloud for embedded into the soft contour of her right breast, just above the nipple, was a welt-red tattoo; an emblem. She rubbed her fingers around and about it, following its delicately etched symmetry, studying its shape and design until the markings became clear. She kneaded the fleshy tissue of her breast and then bombarded the emblem with countless taps and flicks of her fingers, trying to erase the symbol, but it wouldn't go away. The red, cat's paw was there to stay----forever.

Now, memories pounded against her mind. *She remembered.* She recalled the man in black, the gun. Mrs. Landers---dead. She sat up in bed, the stillness pierced by her incessant screams which sounded too big for her face.

The door opened, admitting sunshine and a familiar face, Roscoe.

"It's alright, Brittany," he said gently. "You're safe here. Nothing or no one can harm you now." He yelled over his shoulder. *"Puff!"*

The yellow cat instantly bounded into the room and sprang playfully onto the bed, nestling himself into the crook of the girl's elbow. Puff purred in contentment, licking at Brittany's face. "Meow."

Brittany instinctively stroked the cat as Roscoe fumbled around the room, looking uncomfortable. His impassive face showed no hint off emotion when he noticed the girl's exposed breast and the tell-tale cat's paw. He merely shifted his gaze.

"I'll be back with your breakfast," he mumbled. "Come on, Puff."

159

"Roscoe," Brittany whispered, stopping him. "What is this all about?"

A huge sigh escaped Roscoe's lips. "Maybe later, I'll tell you. First, you eat."

The killings brought about an odd sense of delayed recognition that struck a familiar chord with Sherman, There was a raw boldness surrounding First Ward that could not be explained. It was an eccentric madness that appeared to be customized for that particular neighborhood alone, a halloweenish compulsion for murder that other communities had stubbornly resisted.

What madness! These people were not that type. They were, after all, and, above all----white! Additionally, many of them were civic leaders, CEOs, movers and shakers. Anything, but lunatics. He scoured the database for any extra history of Tilly Schaffner, but there was nothing more. At any rate, Sherman had learned that Schaffner, a former Superior Court Judge in Anniston, Alabama had been born in Dallas, Texas. He had been educated at Harvard and Yale, had graduated with honors. Joined the bench in 1968. He was an outstanding jurist, highly respected by his peers, and was the member of several prestigious country clubs. He was as solid as a rock, Sherman noted, until he moved to First Ward. Now, all of a sudden, the man was the complete opposite. Instead, he now conducted himself like a twenty year old Mack-Daddy straight out of one of those 70s

Blaxploitation movies. Go figure, Sherman chided himself. First Ward had corrupted him.

Sherman pushed the documents away and winked at his guest. "And that was just the part that makes sense." He folded his arms across his chest. "Puff is a part of Winkler, dammit, and I'm telling you that there are countless, little kitty cats out there, just waiting to turn into vicious killers. You get enough of them together and whew, have we got problems."

"Which can only be saved with your laser gun?"

"This is how it all fits. You were there, in charge of the clean-up so I know it shouldn't have escaped your attention. Do you remember the amount of fish dredged from the lake?"

"I remember."

"Do you also remember how countless cats feasted on them right off?"

"Yes."

"The dead fish contaminated the cats."

"But nothing survived Winkler."

"How can you be so sure of that? What if one of those cats survived and over the years have produced offspring who were contaminated who then spread out across the nation. Puff, the cat in Charlotte, may be a survivor of Winkler, a second generation of killer kitties."

"Why aren't their others, then?"

"Who say there's not." Sherman's eyes blazed. "Open your eyes, General. This is Winkler. Puff is a second line of engagement, and there are others like her, literally hundreds, thousands."

"I think you're over-reacting."

"*Over-reacting!?*" Sherman spat disgustedly. "You-you saw how the contaminated fish----trout, bass, what-have-you---took on superpowers that allowed them to live on land with no apparent harm, so you know I'm not lying." He pleaded. "Help me."

"The General softened. "Just a thought or two. What you need is high performance imagery with stereoscopic satellite photographs which allows a view unmolested by the terrain in a way that simple two-dimensional photos never could."

"How clear?"

"Clear enough to peek over a fellow's shoulder and read the label on a box of oatmeal. Presently, the only two companies with the high-spatial resolution imagery equipped with detection, identification, and verification are EarthWatch, and Space Imaging."

"Can you give me a leg up with either of them." When the General shook his head, Sherman persisted. Who else is there?"

"NASA is riding herd on orbital imagery, but it's not commercially available right now." The General waved away any comment or question. "Plus, none of this might be your best bet, and here's why. "Normally, spy satellites circle in one and a half-hour orbits which basically means that if it passed Atlanta on one orbit, the next orbit ninety minutes later would probably show Arkansas because that would represent how far the world has turned in the interval. This being so, your little hot spot in North Carolina wouldn't even be depicted."

"*Dammit!*" Sherman cursed. "I need a frigging spy satellite in place over First Ward. Some strange shit goes on over there every Friday

night, and I want to know exactly what it is and why it's happening."
He dropped his head. "It's just too fucking risky to attempt any type of
surveillance or recon work from ground level, but I still need access to
what's going on down there and to find out who the hell is
responsible." He groaned miserably. "If this is what I think I know it is,
then, sir, we are staring at the prelude of an alien invasion."

Not a word more was spoken.

CHAPTER FOURTEEN

"Lie! Lies! Lies!" Brittany shrieked hysterically. She was crying loudly, pounding the pillows with her fist. Then she was silent, her sad, tear-streaked face staring vacantly at Roscoe, wanting to penetrate the impassive mask that shrouded his countenance. All she felt was billowing clouds of anger, but not at him. She sat quietly, trying to tear away the abrasive emotions that had her so terribly confused. She was unable to think clearly. "Lies," she moaned again through clenched teeth. "My father was not out to destroy you or Puff. The others may have, but not my father, and certainly not my mother." Brittany wiped her eyes. "They didn't have to die."

"They did, though," Roscoe whispered consolingly, "and they intended to kill you. You saw that for yourself." Roscoe shook his head sadly. "It's not over yet, Brittany. Not yet. They'll be back, and they will keep coming back until they have destroyed you, me, and Puff. That's all they now live for, Brittany, to wipe us out. Me. You. Puff."

"*Why!?* Brittany sobbed. "Haven't they killed enough? Why can't they just leave us alone?"

Roscoe heaved a dark, lamented sigh. "Because it doesn't suit their agenda. They can't let it go as long as we are alive." He paused. "I guess it's like when you kill something, you just want to make sure that it is dead. Like a snake. Even after it's lying on the ground, still as can be, you keep right on pounding it because you want to be sure that it's all the way dead. In the back of your mind, you somehow feel that if you kill it all the way, it won't, can't come back to haunt you, and that's what happening with us, Brittany. We have become a part of this thing and they want to make sure that it's dead all the way this time." He grimaced. "Don't think I can explain it no better than that. Understand?"

Trembling, the young girl buried her face in the pillow, whimpering pitifully. "How did me and my family get to be a part of this. Why us?!"

"I ain't got no answer for that, child. I swear I don't." He looked at Puff. "This ol' cat has all the answers. All I know is that she chose you."

Brittany sat upright. "*Chose me!*" She gripped Roscoe's arm tightly. "Please, tell me what's going on, Roscoe. My parents are dead, and there are people that I don't know who want to kill me. I need to know. Please."

Roscoe gripped the girl's hand warmly as he swallowed the lump in his throat. He lifted Puff up. "You see this cat." He dropped Puff on the floor. "Well.......she's dead."

"*Dead!?*"

"Yep, Brittany, ol' Puff is dead. Don't know how to explain it no better than that. That cat is as dead as your mama and papa."

"But I'm looking at her. I've fed her, petted her. Dead things don't eat, remember?"

"You're not making this easy," Roscoe lamented.

"I'm just trying to understand why you're lying to me. I don't have anyone else in the world to turn to and now I'm beginning to see that I can't trust you." Brittany cried into the pillow.

Embracing the girl warmly, Roscoe got an idea. He brightened, gripping her shoulder excitedly. "If something is dead, you can't kill it, right?"

"I guess. How can you kill something that is already dead?"

"Great," he muttered, "I'll be right back." In a flash, Roscoe left the room and returned with a sword which he handed to Brittany. "Look it over real good so you know it's real." When Brittany gave the razor-sharp weapon back to Roscoe, he winked. "Satisfied?" He hefted the sword over his head. "Now, take a good look at Puff," he ordered.

As quick as a flash of lightning, Roscoe swung the sword down fiercely upon the head of the curled-up, sleeping cat. Brittany recoiled in shock. She shrieked in fright, closing her eyes.

"You can open your eyes now," Roscoe chuckled. "Ol' Puff is just fine."

Brittany couldn't believe her eyes. It wasn't possible. There was no blood, no severed head. Just Puff, peacefully snoozing. The sword was broken in half.

Brittany fainted.

When she regained consciousness, Roscoe stuffed a steaming cup of green tea into her hands. "This will soothe your nerves." For the next two minutes, he watched Brittany blow upon the towering steam that rose and hovered over the rim of the cup. Finally, she was able to sip it.

"Any more surprises?"

"That demonstration was the easy part." He wondered where to start. He cleared his throat. "Puff has been dead even before you were born. She died in 64, springtime. I had her ever since she was a baby, before she even opened her eyes, so I was the first thing she saw when she opened those beautiful yellow-green eyes, and from then on, we were together all the way up to the day she died."

"How?'

"Don't rightly know, ain't really tried much too figure it out, but I know she did it for me because that fateful day when I came home and found out from my Mama that we had to move away from First Ward." Roscoe winced. "I remember being madder than I had ever been before. Because I was so young, I didn't even know that kind of hatred existed, but I felt it that day. I felt anger real bad that day.

I ran under the house which was my safe place. Puff, of course, was with me, and it was that day that I asked a favor of my cat."

"Wh-what do you ask Puff for?"

"To me, I was just saying something." Roscoe wiped away a tear. "I-I didn't know."

"Roscoe," Brittany said firmly, "what did you ask of Puff?"

"I-I asked Puff, my dearly beloved cat, to come back to life when she died to kill white people. That same day," Roscoe moaned, "Puff went out and died, came back to do exactly what I had asked of her."

"To kill white people?"

Roscoe nodded. "Yeah."

Brittany pointed at herself. "I'm white, but Puff saved me. I don't know how she did or why. I just know that a man was about to shoot me and then I saw Puff. Just before I fainted, I remember thinking that I was going to be alright.

"You're a special girl, Brittany. Maybe Puff understood that you were different. Animals have this insight, I don't know what it is, but Puff likes you. In a way," Roscoe grinned, "I guess that makes you the High Priestess of First Ward. Just think about it. Puff has this amazing ability to heal your wounds, she'll fight all your battles-----."

"But she can't bring my parents back."

Roscoe was silent.

Brittany cried.

"The evil men that killed your Ma and Pa won't get away with it. Puff won't let them. I promise you that."

On Monday, when the TEU detachment arrived in Charlotte, they listened sympathetically to Sherman's emotional harangue about the need to find the cat without delay, but none of the men budged.

"What fucking kind of pigwash is this?" Sherman ranted. "Wait until tomorrow. What's in heaven's name is wrong with right now? There's still a lot of daylight left. This stinks and don't give me that crap about this being a holiday because who gives a shit about Martin Luther King's birthday?"

"You're right, sir. It has nothing to do with any holiday but we need time to prepare the equipment. We must acquaint ourselves with the radiation quotient of this city because certain chemicals such as benzene may trigger the sensor and we just might mistake the cat for something else." A.D. Darling looked at Sherman. "We need to do some geological testing. Every city has a radiation quotient consistent with its hazardous waste sites and the pollutants in the air. Through a process of ionizing radiation----."

"Sounds like an educated mouthful of bullshit to me," Sherman bellowed. "Isn't this the same doggone laser used to detect where Nana, the lion that escaped from the zoo, was?"

"It is, sir, but what you have to keep in mind," A.D. Darling pontificated, "is that Nana was alive, a living, breathing creature that we were able to detect with thermal imaging. Your cat, this Puff, is dead so there is no body heat so thermal imaging-----"

"Is worthless. I don't want any thumb-twiddling from TEU. I expect you guys to be aggressive in carrying out your mission and I have your asses back on a plane out of here in a week." Sherman slowed his breathing down. "Is a week asking too much?"

"Since Puff has no body heat being that the animal is dead, we'll adjust the specs of the laser to detect her according to the chemicals makeup of her body composition so," A.D. Darling scowled, "I will need the toxic samples taken from the area where Mr. Brown lived as a child."

Sherman scratched his head. "Did you leave anything out? If not, I'll see you, gents, first thing in the morning. Bright and early.

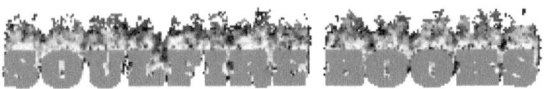

Outside, it started to snow and Puff walked slower, her belly sagging, drooping towards fat. The rims of her eyes were thin, scarlet-red, her body coat sallow and for once, she felt exhausted; vulnerable. She recognized the signs by instinct. Soon, her power would dissipate and she would be called back to the grave. Just like before. Inside her brain, she knew she would have to get away, go off alone---to die. *But there was still time.* She still yet had time to assemble all her power for one final attack against those who hated her master-----and new mistress. The cat turned sad, but tried to console herself with the fact that she would, one day, return and that they---Roscoe and Brittany---would be waiting. Always. Forever together. One.

The girl was Puff's gift to Roscoe.

In the shimmering distance of McDowell Street, the glistening sidewalks gleamed like polished stones and Puff crossed over, stopping to rest under a teal green Audi. She purred, then moved on. Alerted by noise, she sauntered lazily towards the sound of the blaring horn. Kids out for a drive. She bypassed them, the foul stench of stale beer assaulting her central nervous system, padlocking her olfactory senses. Puff hated that stink.

But it wasn't just that. She was tired, physically fatigued. She took a few more rapid steps, then stumbled, an apparent loss of control. She experienced a slight bout of dizziness and acute stinging in her eyes, blurring her vision. She meowed softly as a brutal gust of wind lifted her up, moving her, slamming her into a brick wall. Her limp became more pronounced.

This was just like the last time. She was in regression, and she was declining fast. She had to rest, conserve energy, multiply her strength. *She still had time.*

At Myers Street, she knelt under the cold shadow of a trash can and tried to shake off her fatigue, to reinvigorate herself, but she couldn't.

Suddenly, someone trudged down the street. A young boy. He was slouched over inside a huge, black overcoat, his pale face haunted by deep, hollowed out eyes ringed in heavy, black mascara; his spiked, multi-colored hair softened by snow. Smudges of cold air formed mushroom vapors, squeezing out his ebony-painted lips, over and around his bubble-gum.

Instantly, Puff was all over him, raking his face, leaving shreds of bloody skin hanging off his chin like a peeled, unripe banana. Shards of electric fire pumped through the sinews and muscles of the cat, switching ON unused power, ad with unequalled vigor, Puff bit and tore into the boy's body, ripping out whole chunks of flesh. The boy's painful screaming only spurred the cat on, inducing more frenzy. She chewed off one ear, spat it out. Then the other. In a fit of wanton glee, Puff sprang atop the boy's pastel-colored head with its bed of spikes, and pecking with a single, piercing claw perforated his brain. Ignoring the yells, she pried the top of the boy's head off as if it was a lid and then, with reckless relish, began to eat her way down into his skull, consuming the squishy, mushy, gray matter with absolute gusto.

Puff felt good.

Near the Eleventh Street exit, next to the highway, the red Jeep pulled in, music loud, the occupants of the vehicle reeking of beer and reefer. The Jeep turned in, made a U-turn and then raced back towards I-77.

"Get out of the way, stupid cat," the driver yelled.

From a back window, an empty bottle sailed out, shattering into a thousand broken fragments at Puff's head. A second bottle flew from the window, also crashing loudly into bits. The red Jeep sped onto the Interstate.

"I bet I gave that cat a heart attack," the man in the back remarked, laughing wildly.

"Fucker will probably be scared Jeeps for the rest of its life."

"MEOW!"

"Oh shit!" the driver yelled, mortified. "Look!"

"What the------?"

"I-I don't believe this," the man in the back seat cried. "Step on the gas."

The speedometer jumped to 80 and the image of the cat faded.

"Whew," gasped the driver, shaking his head. "For a second, I thought that bullshit cat was chasing us. Boy, was that some good weed or what? Roll down the window. We need to clear our fucking heads."

"MEOW!"

"Oh God, no!" the driver shouted as Puff rammed into the side of the vehicle, making it skid almost out of control. "This ain't no high. This shit real."

"Step on it.'

85 MPH

The cat still ran alongside.

90 MPH

Puff. Still there.

"MEOW!" She rammed the vehicle again. And again.

"Help us, dear Jesus, please," someone in the Jeep prayed as Puff thundered into the

side of the Jeep again. BOOM!

"Go faster or else the damn thing is going to ram us again."

But this time, Puff didn't thunder into the speeding, red Jeep. Instead, she merely swiped the back-end, spinning it sideways, sending it careening into the median, over the guardrail and downwards.

Puff felt great, her strength returning, but despite this vigorous physical upheaval, she knew that it wouldn't last and that she wouldn't last and that soon she would be driven into retreat due to her oncoming weakness.

Ignoring the instincts to conserve energy, she knew she had to ride this power surge to annihilate her enemies before the sanctions of her own decomposing body would be imposed upon her. *She had to respond now.*

Her intuition sharpened by the promise of death, she willingly accepted it with casual indifference, but still, she had to destroy the men who had raised their hands against her beloved master, Roscoe. From now on, everything she did would have to revolve around protecting him and crushing anyone that might threaten his future security. The world must never harm him. Ever.

Puff gave herself a bath. With slow, deliberate strokes of her rough tongue, the cat moisturized her yellow coat until it was wet and glistening. Suddenly, she beautiful again. It had been a long time since she had known that feeling dating back to the moment she had returned, arriving on Roscoe's doorsteps, polished and exquisitely fabulous.

The purring stopped. The yellow cat had no desire to go back. She didn't want to leave Roscoe again. In a quiet flash, she darted away.

Puff was almost home.

Once there, she dashed under the bed, her soft footsteps receding until she had curled herself up in her favorite item of Roscoe's clothing, a caramel-colored sweatshirt that smell heavily of her master and Egyptian Musk. Inhaling the sweet vapors, the pangs became more acute, getting progressively more debilitating. Then she couldn't breathe and a powerful wave of nausea shot throughout the length of her body, crippling her as her legs gave way. She crumpled to the floor, her ears ringing with a feverish din. Slimy mucous dripped from her nose. This wasn't hunger. This was vulnerability.

But it was also something else.

CHAPTER FIFTEEN

7 days later.

"What this does," The TEU technician explained calmly, pointing to a control panel is----."

BeepBeepBeep....

"Wh-what just happened?" Sherman begged excitedly to know, clutching the tech's shoulder.

"You just got lucky, sir. We're getting warm."

"Warm? What does that mean? Getting warm?"

"It means your fucking target-----."

"You mean Puff!"

"Who else," A.D. Darling announced. "We're close enough to smell her shit."

"Hot damn!" Sherman exclaimed, clapping his hands.

BeepBeepBeep.

"Turn around and go back," Darling ordered. "Don't worry," he said to Sherman, "there is no escape now for the cat now that we've got her tracked."

Heading in the opposite direction, the beeps grew fainter, then stopped, the red indicator light switched OFF.

"Pull over into that parking lot." Darling addressed Sherman. "I have heard enough of your destructive obsession with this cat, so I can automatically guess what comes next, but once I pinpoint the direct location of your target, our job here is done."

"And it will be a job well done," Sherman beamed. "Brilliant. You'll be commended. Count on it." He punched the driver's shoulder. "Just show me where they're hiding."

"First," Darling quipped, "some advice."

"Advice?" Sherman sounded insulted. "Advice! You've done your job and I appreciate it, but I don't want or need your advice."

"But I think you should reconsider------."

"Damn you, Darling. Don't you see I don't like you. I think you're obnoxious and pompous, and I was beginning to doubt your abilities when you failed to locate the cat from the air, and I'll have you know that you have barely redeemed yourself." Sherman turned up his nose. "Advice from your kind. Not hardly."

"At any rate, sir, I would feel better if I offer it. It's more ethical than personal or professional, and yes, the feeling is mutual. I can't stand your guts either."

"Now that it's officially established that we don't sit horses, stop beating around the bush and get it off your chest, whatever it is that's eating you."

"Very well. You may want to consider asking my superiors to loan you this sensor. I haven't the authority to leave it myself."

Sherman laughed. "If that is all, then you can pack your equipment and vamoose. I doubt if I'll need you."

"Something else you should consider-----."

"Aren't you finished yet?

"-----is that in addition to its tracking function," Darling continued, "the sensor has been equipped with a Spectra 4 Toxin Prohibitor which cripples the immune system of your cat, thereby weakening it. For example, Spectra 4 went silently into effect even before the red light had started beeping, alerting me to the fact that we were within two hundred yards of the cat. This was done so that if something went wrong and we were detected, the cat would be in such a weakened state that it couldn't do any real damage. Once I heard of the awesome destructive power of the animal, I took the extra precaution in the event the cat attacked us, or you, against my wishes, attacked the cat."

"Fuck you and your wishes," Sherman spat in contempt.

"Nevertheless, it was done. I felt that TEU needed protection from both of you animals."

"You're a white coat, lab rat. I don't respect your advice."

"Listen carefully, sir. I don't figure you to be the most intelligent person in the world, so I'm telling you to use Spectra 4. I would like to believe that you don't plan to try to be a hero because playing Rambo will, nine times out of ten, get you killed."

"One more time for the road," Sherman commented flatly, "fuck you." Then, he looked away, but turned once more to face Darling. "You really want to know what my beef is with you white coats. You want to make everything more complicated than it is, but just for the dag-blamed record, I want you to know that Puff is no match for me." He grinned widely. "I got the laser from SDI," he said proudly.

Darling painstakingly described what could possibly go wrong with the complicated and expensive SDI laser. Most, he explained, were not impeccable and had been assessed with disturbingly low lab norms which could be ineffective against the high level of toxicity he believed the cat's immune system possessed. "Right now," he patiently lectured, "while just sitting here, Spectra has the cat so weak, you could literally walk up to the bastard, lift up her tail and fuck her." Darling beamed. "I'll eagerly stake my reputation on that, sir."

Sherman sat tall in the seat. "Read my lips." Even though the pair were cracked, chafed, and blistered, the silent message was clear. "*NO!*"

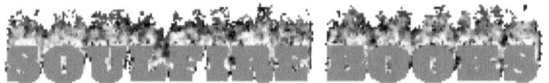

Shortly thereafter.

Suffering greatly, Puff dragged herself to the window, she leaped on the back of a chair and pressed her aching face to the glass pane. She vomited on the curtains. But outside she saw the van with the men in it slow down. One pointed at the house where she was, then sped off. No doubt, that van was the source of her pain. Though, she understood the danger, she was much too weak to chase the vehicle down to kill the occupants. Her stomach heaved and green, watery vomit spewed out of her mouth. Too depleted to move, she laid in it.

"meow." The sound was barely audible.

Business had been slow today, so Bradley McNeil scribbled a few more entries in his account ledger and shoved both it and the security deposits notebook into the safe, and nonchalantly gave the combination lock a satisfying spin. He then crossed over to the wet bar and fixed himself a drink, He started out of his home office, remembered he had left the desk lamp on, so he retraced his steps and flicked the lamp's switch from ON to OFF.

Nursing his scotch on the rocks, he decided on a cold sandwich. *Turkey and cheese on rye.* Several steps from the kitchen, he sensed vibrations, not discernible enough to be called noise or even sound, but enough of a distraction to disrupt the stillness of the house. He didn't dwell on it as long as it wasn't mice.

At the entrance to the kitchen, he struggled to keep a straight face as he tossed back the remainder of his drink, the searing liquor burned his throat, then fanned out into a pleasant smoothness that laced his throat with a soothing tingle.

Combing his long, brown hair out of his brown eyes with his hands, he removed the sandwich fixings from the fridge and reached into the pantry for bread. *He froze.* This time, sound, although unintelligible clashed with the noiselessness. He waited on his ears to cash in on the sound, but it became mute, hushing itself up. *Ssshh!*

He returned to his meal. Brandishing a thick slab of cheese and a loaf or two of lettuce, he plopped them down upon the open face of the bread and carved off a hefty slice of meat. The overhead light flickered, spat electricity, dimmed, went OFF, sputtered back ON, finally expiring, leaving the room in black darkness.

"Damn!"

On top of the pantry was a flashlight. He grabbed it angrily, unlocked the cellar door and stormed heavily down the stairs to the fuse box. He cut a wide swatch through the darkness, following the beam of light until he reached the tiny, subterranean alcove where the box protruded from a niche in the wall. He quickly re-set the switch, flipping it UP. *Lights.* Slamming the cover shut, he hurriedly raced to the stairs, ascended them noisily and returned to the warmth of the kitchen.

He nearly pissed on himself.

"Good evening, sir," the young, blonde girl said sweetly, "I'm Brittany. High Priestess."

"Ho-How did you get in here?" McNeil stammered. "Who are you and what do you want?"

"You have trespassed upon the scared grounds of First Ward."

"I don't know what you are talking about. I own this townhouse." McNeil was impressed with the confidence in his voice, the logic of his argument. "I don't know about any holy ground, but I do know who the trespassers are, and I'm looking at both of them. I'll excuse the cat." He tapped his foot playfully at Puff. "I'm a peace-loving man so I just hope you will accept my invitation to just leave and not come back. Leave now and there'll be no police."

"I'm sorry," Roscoe boomed, "and you are the one who must leave."

"And the punishment for your trespassing," Brittany acknowledged, "is death."

The knife was in Roscoe's hand before McNeil even saw it. The white man recoiled in fear, but before he could react, the long blade had been plunged into his chest. Only the shiny, black hilt of the blade rested above his immaculately pressed shirt.

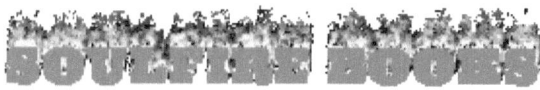

Time curled up its toes and became the other side of midnight. Thunder coughed and rain, like snotty phlegm, dripped from runny-nosed clouds while on Fifth Street, an old woman died in her sleep, and a few blocks west, another. Death, like a fatal strain of bacteria, was circulating in First Ward. It was silent. Strong. Accelerating.

Rosie Kroger discovered she couldn't breathe so well, and in a townhouse overlooking the rain-soaked pavement of the central tennis court, Matthew Thompson's face turned from being skeptical to being quizzical. What the hell was going on. Having no answer for himself, his expression cork-screwed into another design----horror. *The cat wasn't dead!* Six shots to its head----and it just sat there. Purring.

As loudly as he could, he screamed.

Through the walls, Vinny thought he heard a scream so he sat up in bed, listening. "It's alright," he consoled his boss' wife, "just some dumb jerk with too much to drink. That's all it is. Go back to watching the TV."

Again. The scream.

"That was a scream, Vinny," the woman protested. "Don't you think you should check it out?"

Vinny didn't want to, but he got up just the same, slipping on his trousers and pulling his silk robe tightly about him. He leaned over the bed, kissing the woman's lips.

"Get ready for round 2 when I get back." He stalked to the front door, thinking that perhaps he should let the cops handle this. Then again, it probably wasn't a real scream to begin with. He would feel like such a jerk if his neighbor was into kinky sex and he interrupted them.

Still, he knocked loudly on the door. There was no response, so he pounded harder. Still no answer. Having felt that he had discharged his duty, Vinny went home.

"Wouldn't you know it," he explained to the woman, Tess, as he returned to his bedroom. "The bum wouldn't come to the door." He chuckled. "Maybe next time, "I'll ask if I can't join in. A little S&M will liven up any bedroom, I guarantee you that. Hey, doll, what's the matter? Cat got your tongue or something?" He got no response. "Don't many broads get in Vinny the Stallion's bed and want to sleep."

Vinny quietly slipped between the covers of the cool, satin sheets. "Wake up, woman." He rolled over on top of the woman, planting a wet kiss upon her lips. "Damn," Vinny exclaimed, "this dame is beautiful." He moved his right hand to her breast and felt sticky wetness through the thin, sheer fabric of her nightie. The gooey moisture coated his finger under his nose, and initially all he smelled was the fragrance of raw sex, then he vaguely caught a whiff of some other odor, but for reason, could not detect what it was. Then, it hit him-------Blood!

Quickly, he threw himself off the inert body and fumbled with the switch on the nightstand. He frantically depressed the button. It clicked, but no light. He clicked again, hearing the metallic ding, but yet there was still no illumination.........except for—what was that? From out of a far corner of the bedroom, over near his Nautilus machine, there were two streams of penetrating green-yellow light. The lights were moving, coming closer.

The scary, twin beams of light came nearer, moving eerily slow.

Then, without warning, the lights popped ON!

"What? A stupid cat!" Vinny muttered after seeing Puff.

"But a very special cat," the blonde girl spoke.

Vinny rubbed his eyes. "Where did you come from?" he gasped.

"That is no real concern of yours," Roscoe boomed. "What is important is where did you come from? You shouldn't be here. Her either." Roscoe nodded his head at the bed.

Vinny stared at Tess and shrieked wildly. The entire left side of her chest had been ripped open. She was dead.

Roscoe resumed talking. "This place is hallowed and your presence has defiled it."

"Do not fear The Reaper," Brittany chanted, edging close to the terrified man. "No one can save you, and for your sins, you must give the devil his due.

Brittany thrust the knife in deeply, giving the blade a savage twist to help cut through his jugular and to slash through the windpipe. She was momentarily mesmerized by the manner by which the bright, red blood gushed forth from his neck like a geyser.

This was her first kill!

For days on end, the kill bothered Brittany and she tried to suppress her guilt, but no matter how hard she tried, she couldn't seem to shake the unrelenting regret that dogged her every waking moment. In the early morning, it would rear its ugly head and use her conscience as a pulpit from which to stir up her remorse or to agitate her self-loathing.

She had killed a man! She was no High Priestess. She was Brittany McCall, murderess. Since she had been a little girl, she had deemed herself one of mankind's saviors, but now overwhelming evidence condemned her hypocrisy since, with her own hands, she had destroyed a life. In some unfathomable way, she couldn't be sure who to blame, but she knew that it had all started with Puff.

So impressed with this recognition, she accepted it verbatim. *Puff was responsible.* Instinctively, she knew not to trespass beyond this threatening acknowledgement, knowing that anything further might entitle her to the wrath of the cat, so she was vehemently opposed to subjecting herself to even the thought----much less the actual act of betrayal.

Brittany shook with fear.

Calming herself, the fractured image of her brother displayed itself before her mind's eye and for the first time, she didn't look away. She refused to blink as other images emerged out of hiding and blazed into view. Gaining confidence, she studied the passing faces of her parents, both now dead, and understood that it was Puff who was at the root of their deaths. Of that, she was certain.

"Everything would still be just fine," she sobbed, "if it wasn't for Puff." Abruptly, she detested the yellow cat. She also understood what she must do.

Oh shit!

CHAPTER SIXTEEN

Today---SuperBowl Sunday----was the only day of the year that Roscoe would take a drink, Only beer. He had already had two during the pre-game show, so he was feeling festive. Brittany had gone for a walk and he was glad because she had been a bit annoying lately. He also didn't know where Puff was, but was expecting her to come bounding in at any moment, disturbing him. She had been a little antsy all morning, filled with a sort of kinetic energy as if something was wrong, but that also was annoying. Roscoe didn't like to be messed with on SuperBowl Sunday.

Later for both Brittany and Puff, Roscoe thought. It was kick-off time! Green Bay had won the coin toss and had elected to receive the ball. Roscoe popped the top of another brew. Here came the kick. It was a long, high one and the stadium crowd howled and cheered wildly as the football turned end-over-end, sailing through the air. It was caught deep in Packer territory and the fans went wild when the two teams made punishing contact with each other. They cheered.

Then.

Another very loud cheer, but Roscoe had to fend off surprise because the cheer was not coming from the television or from the crowd in San Diego. This cheer of frenzy was near, at his elbow; close.

Sherman batter-rammed the door down and then stormed the apartment, firing two, quick shots in succession at his target. The first bullet tore through Roscoe's brain, but the second one was swatted away by Puff who magically appeared out of nowhere.

The yellow cat roared ferociously, tearing into the arm of a soldier who tried to intercept her. "Oh my God!" he yelled.

Sherman fell back in retreat, cursing loudly and screaming commands as Puff leaped for the throat of another of his men. While the cat licked the blood off the face of her dead master, Sherman and his men dashed outside to the Jeep where an almond-colored soldier manned a giant laser gun.

As soon as Puff leaped through the doorway, the man trained the laser at the cat and squeezed the trigger, drawing a direct hit with the invisible beam. Puff staggered, momentarily disabled by the five second blast. Sherman held up his hand, the signal to cease fire. He smiled smugly as the cat toppled over in the dirt, unmoving. Sherman bobbed his head at another soldier who moved cautiously forward.

"Cover him," Sherman ordered the almond-colored man.

Standing over the lifeless body of the fallen yellow feline, the soldier gently prodded the still body with the toe of his boot, then he howled in anguish. Puff ripped his leg off.

"Fire! Fire! Sherman screamed frantically at the gunnery sergeant who aimed the gun at the cat as she stumbled to her feet. He fired. Puff shook it off. "Crank it up to full power," Sherman yelled. But the man was much too slow. Puff tore his heart out.

Sherman ran to his Jeep.

Bounding to the ground, Puff turned her back to the scattering, fleeing soldiers and sprayed them with urine. Instantly, they were incapacitated, coughing and gasping for air, writhing in uncontrollable agony, twisting and squirming in pain.

Puff searched for Sherman who had bowled over in a tight knot at the front of his Jeep. Spying the approach of the cat, his eyes grew wide in terror, but instead of begging, Sherman awkwardly steeled himself and pulled himself upright., steadying himself by using the Jeep as a brace. He clawed desperately for his sidearm and, at once, recognized how useless it was. Still, he fired the weapon, but the bullets had no effect whatever, not even fazing the creature. He fell back against the Jeep, a whimper escaping his lips.

Puff crashed her tail into Sherman's ankles, crushing the bone to powder. Sherman, quite naturally, crumpled to the ground, howling in pain while behind him, there was the anxious scrambling of his men, regaining their feet, running away.

"Help me!" Sherman called out.

None listened.

Help me!

The cat's tail smashed into Sherman's back and red-hot pain rocketed up and down his spine as Puff methodically whipped him, each vertebrae cracking and snapping loudly. Sherman's pitiful screams rent the air, but just prior to him losing consciousness, he was flipped over onto his broken back. He yelped helplessly, gazing into a tranquil, Carolina blue sky.

Puff straddled Sherman's neck, stuffing her long tail down the man's throat, shutting OFF his breath. His windpipe heaved, seeming to catch fire. Sherman couldn't breathe and finally, his lungs exploded.

Puff bellowed. "MEOW!"

CHAPTER SEVENTEEN

Roscoe was dead!

And for the next five days, mayhem followed. Charlotte was in absolute panic and chaos. Unable to quell the rebellion of the yellow cat, the city was wrecked as Puff angrily destroyed everyone and everything that crossed her path. Her sporadic violence escalated as she clashed with and attacked police. Citizens, fearing for their lives, fled the city in droves, seeking shelter from the wrath of the cat.

More than a quarter of CMPD had been sent out against the cat and after all of them had died, the Mayor appealed to the President, and within hours, on Friday the 30th, a state of emergency was declared in Mecklenburg County. The National Guard was called in.

The entire nation was galvanized, glued to their TVs, shocked by the brutal, destructive power of a seemingly harmless house cat. It just didn't make any sense. When news footage graphically ran shots of houses, cars, and men that had been consumed by the fury of the yellow cat, it just didn't seem possible. How could such a thing as this even be possible?

In the meantime Puff continued her vicious onslaught unabated, unchecked. The National Guard proved no match and they, as had the local police, died horrible deaths. By evening, the cat's stranglehold on the enfeebled city was almost total as she seemed to be everywhere at once, squatting on every road, killing whatever got her attention.

Night fell.

On Saturday, the cat withdrew from the SouthPark area, but my mid-morning occupied the deserted campus of Pfeifer University, causing millions of dollars worth of damage before lunging up Park Road, heading back into the inner city.

Near Ericsson Stadium at 300 Stonewall Street, Puff's ears perked up. *Music!* And in a fit of frenzied passion, she gnawed her way silently through the door of the dance club. Inside, the noise was much louder and she followed the sound like it was an aroma. To the left of a hidden balcony were a short flight of stairs that guided Puff to a small, dark dance floor where the walls were mirrored and where romantic nooks were carved out of the smoky wood, but the music was not here. To the right, a spiral staircase beckoned and Puff slowly ascended. She moved silently until she saw them through the glass. At the roof top bar, a pair of men sat close, holding hands, sipping a shared drink as they wistfully glared into the sparkling lights of a huge aquarium. Puff settled back on her haunches, wiggling her behind, getting ready to pounce. She inched closer, but the rainbow-colored, tropical birds in their cages squawked loudly, alerting the lovers to the approaching presence.

Puff sprang!

The force of the attack drove the larger of the two men off his stool, spread-eagling him backwards onto the polished bar counter. Puff chewed out his eyes. The other man grappled with Puff, trying vainly to dislodge the animal from the face of his companion, but with a swat of her tail. Puff sent the man sailing through the air, crashing into a stack of chairs. She returned to her feast, nibbling at the nose and carving off one of the man's ears as if it was a slice of Thanksgiving turkey, and when she tired of these dry morsels of meat, she kicked out the man's teeth to provide easier access to the glistening saliva-filled tongue, a moist sliver of a delicacy. Piercing the wet cut of meat down its creased center, the yellow cat sucked greedily, slurping up, savoring the pulpy juices within.

Puff was sated.

Around this time, the second man---the smaller-- thought he had made it. He fled the terrace, hearing the haunting screams of his lover and ran out onto the roof and jumped in the elevator. It descended.

The man stopped it between floors, suspended between the roof and the cellar. Feeling secure, he slumped into a perspiring sweaty heap. He sighed wearily, believing the cat could not find him, and the passing minutes compelled him to feel even more secure. The cat did not know where he was. Praises be!

Meanwhile, perched atop the elevator, Puff slowly went on and on, biting carefully through the coiled skin of the thick, steel-wired pulley that hoisted the elevator through the shaft. The tense outer strands unraveled, snapping one by one until none were left to support the cabin, and with a mighty crash, the elevator plummeted to the cellar, the ornate wood paneling and steel beams caving in upon the smaller man, Leo Bartley, who died quickly enough.

The yellow cat left.

Behind The Coffee Cup on Clarkson Street, the cat meandered below the football stadium and then went to find Brittany.

By noon, ten more people in The Queen City of Charlotte had bit the dust.

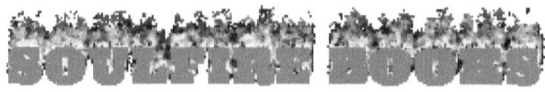

The pattern of the carnage did not vary over the weekend. In fact, it intensified as the power of the yellow cat increased, and it became so severe that the President ordered all armed forces on standby as he prepared to commence an aerial evacuation of Charlotte after which, he intended the bomb the city.

At 2:15 EST, he got an urgent phone call.

"Mr. President, this is A.D. Darling of the Army Technical Escort Unit out in Utah.....Yes sir, that is correct, sir.....I think I may have a solution to the problem in Charlotte....I wouldn't bet my life on it, but it's worth a try.....No, that's not an inconvenience to me, and yes, I can leave right away. Good day, Mr. President.

2 hours later

Each member of The Joint Chiefs of Staff seemed to be speaking at once, and in different languages because each man had his own personal agenda, and in no time at all, Darling was made to feel he was the odd man out. None of these old war horses were truly concerned about the welfare of Charlotte since their major concern appeared to be how to stay one step ahead of the other members of the JCOS while his concern was with killing the cat.

Having inherited the crisis, Darling was ready to move ahead with a controlled, unified effort quickly. His plan was to move, strike fast, kill the cat. Simple.

The Generals had other plans. One of them said. "I'm dead set against deploying ground troops. Too risky, and I don't think the American public is going to stand by and let us commit more soldiers to what has already proven to be a waste of manpower."

"But what about the civilian population down there? What are they going to do when they run out of supplies? What about the need to eat?" Darling was incensed.

"Then they venture out at their own peril. If a damned hot-dog is worth the risk of death, then there's going to be one less person for us to fret over. That may sound harsh, my boy, but when you're the US military, you know that war is not amusing and in case you haven't heard, my boy, war is hell."

"No offense, sir," Darling protested, "but I'm telling you that Spectra does not work through the air. It has already been tried. The cat has to be tracked from the ground. There is no other way."

"In a war, my boy, you improvise." The General winked slyly at Darling. "Most of the prep work has already been done for you, so all you need now do is to shut up and to listen." He motioned to an inconspicuous aide who, without delay, dimmed the lights. "Now, here's the plan."

The Plan! Darling felt as if he had been betrayed, and when the overhead projector whirred ON, he knew that the hard-headed ghost of the late General Sherman was still alive and well because the General exemplified his foolhardy spirit.

"What you are seeing, my boy," General Perkins narrated, "is a shot of uptown Charlotte as viewed from a Spot-1 satellite." He fussed over the clarity, muttering mainly to himself. Still, not quite satisfied, he switched imaging. "Now," he conceded, "this is much better." He pointed to another aerial shot. "And this is the neighborhood adjacent to uptown. Note," he marveled, "at the vivid crispness of the photo's one-meter precision. Magnificent. At any rate, this Wilmore neighborhood is of immediate significance to us because it is here," he pointed, "that we intend to lure the cat, and let you, Mr. Darling, do your part in the plan."

"Which is?"

"To cripple the cat's immune system. Isn't that what you told the Commander-In-Chief that you could do?"

"But what about the people that live in that community?"

"We will airlift them out, and then the rest should be easy."

"It is my understanding, sir," Darling contended, "that the cat has been spotted frequently in the neighborhood where it was raised and his master born."

"First Ward, you must mean?"

"If the cat is there as indicated," Darling Insisted, "why lure her from where she is known to be to somewhere else? I don't get it. Why not bombs away in First Ward?"

Perkins grunted nasally. "Economics, my boy, is the name of that tune," He flicked to another aerial image that contained beautiful homes, tree-lined streets, and fancy cars." "First Ward," he lectured. Then he switched the images back to Wilmore. He grunted again. "Get the picture. The government plunked down 41 million dollars to gentrify First Ward and Uncle Sam wants his investment protected at all costs, if that is possible."

"So, Wilmore is the-----."

"My God, my boy," Perkins scoffed, "what is there to save in this picture?" He pointed at the screen. "Just look for yourself. This is what is called The South End down there in Charlotte. Now, if you cross the tracks, you're in Wilmore. Quite an eyesore compared even to its sister community, South End. Plus, they can rebuild, for goodness sakes, or as it is already being considered, the city wants to build an uptown baseball stadium over there when this is finished."

Darling laughed aloud.

"Don't act so self-righteous," Perkins snapped. "Even in times of war, plans must be made for its aftermath. How do you think France and Britain bounced back after the devastation of World War 2?' Perkins huffed. "We have a plan for Wilmore and it will be performed accordingly. Personally, I don't give a hoot if they build a baseball field or a brothel there, it's not really my concern." He stared at Darling. "How do we lure the cat to Wilmore?"

"Gentleman," Darling announced solemnly, "we have a problem."

The Joint Chiefs of Staff glanced knowingly at one other.

"I don't know how to lure the cat anywhere. As I keep telling you, Spectra is useless from the air. Therefore it must be controlled from ground level, meaning we have to put boots on the ground, and face the yellow cat eye-to-eye." He winked at Perkins. "Isn't this the kind of in-fighting that you guys live for?'

"Okay, I get it," Perkins snarled. "If you are that damned confident in the infallibility of Spectra, I would be more than happy to drop you from a plane within striking distance of the cat. Are you, Mr. Darling, willing to take that risk?"

Darling swallowed hard, but was silent.

"Aha," Perkins exclaimed "Amazing, isn't it, what a bit of reality can accomplish? You say you weakened the cat, but did you know for sure? Certainly not. And yes, you can track the cat as you have so aptly demonstrated, but did you-----can you-----verify that the cat's system was weakened?"

"No sir."

"Well, do you have any proof whatever that the cat was in any way fazed by Spectra?"

"No sir, I do not."

"Then all you have is conjecture, am I right, Mr. Darling? You don't know, do you?" He screwed his face up in disgust. "So, truthfully, you are no more reliable with your Spectra than Sherman was with his laser that got him killed. That's my problems with white coats, you guys run a few tests and start patting each other on the backs even before you've proven a damned thing except that the thing will work if you insert batteries." He turned to face Darling. "Can you guarantee the safety of troops if we committed them to a ground attack?"

Darling was honest. "No."

"Then, gentlemen, we revert back to Plan A immediately."

"Oh my God," Darling yelped. They were going to bomb the entire city of Charlotte with the people in it. "Oh my God!"

Behind him, the inconspicuous aide aimed a gun at the back of Darling's head. "You will come with me, Mr. Darling. Peacefully, I hope."

"They did what!?" the Mayor exclaimed hotly.

"That's right. It's just came in. *For-your-eyes-only.*"

"But they wouldn't," the Mayor shouted.

"They did, sir. They have countermanded the Order of the President."

"This can't be," the Mayor sat down. "No, this can't be," shaking his head in disbelief. "This can't be happening." He looked up sadly. "What does this leave us with?"

"Barely enough time to get ready to evacuate, and that courtesy only applies to you and your staff, family members, and from what I'm led to understand, that is a grudging concession."

The Mayor pounded his desk with his fist. "What do they expect me to do, to just run out of the city and not to alert everyone. Well, I'm going public."

"Y-you can't do that, sir. All hell would break loose. There would be widespread pandemonium and panic. Can you imagine what would erupt if you went public with the news that the city was about to be devastated by a bombing sortie?"

"Set everything up at once," the Mayor said, ignoring the remarks. "I'll broadcast from here."

When the phone rang, the aide hastily answered, then looked at the Mayor. "It's General Perkins. He wants to know if you've accepted his offer to be airlifted out?"

"I'll take that," the Mayor stated flatly, yanking the phone from the aide's grasp. "Hello, General Perkins, this is the Mayor of Charlotte." He paused. "*Go to hell!*"

First, no one in the Charlotte metropolitan area could believe what they were hearing. This couldn't be right what the Mayor was saying. It just couldn't be. No way! Then, slowly, with a sense of dreaded finality, the reality commenced to sink in. *They were all going to die!*

Within minutes, the fear deepened and spread, and out of this morass, despair took root, and following this---complete and total pandemonium. Residents of the city sought to leave, to flee, and in the ensuing mayhem, countless people were crushed in car crashes, each vehicle vying for as much road space as possible. And then there was Puff. The still bitter creature was everywhere, from the top of the town to the bottom, terrible in her merciless slaughter.

Largely through the violence of the cat alone, an entire Eastside neighborhood was wiped out completely, and more died in the adjoining communities from the sheer fright of knowing the yellow cat was so close by.

Chaos reigned supreme.

Not even nominally afraid, Brittany knew she had to do something. She had since returned to First Ward to the townhouse owned by her family. Staring blankly at the expiring time ticking steadily OFF across the screen of the TV set, she tried to concentrate.

45 minutes.

She felt the pressure. It scalded her brain, striking at her ability to think clearly, shrinking her focus down to absolute zero. At twenty past the hour, her heart faltered as she failed to gain coherent thought. All her senses seemed arrested; frozen, and within seconds, this paralyzing inertia branched out, seeping into other regions of her body, shutting down the smaller systems. She crumbled to the floor.

38 minutes left.

For the most part, she saw no need to get up as time seemed to pass much quicker and faster than it routinely seemed to do. She already felt cut off from everything. Already, she felt dead.

34 minutes more.

Each fleeting second added its own brand of misery to the final, closing chapter of her life. At almost precisely 3:27, she recalled, in vivid color, her mother dressing her in pink for Easter. She had been three. Seconds later, grainy images of her brother flashed by; such a handsome kid. At round about 3:30, she saw her father's stern look when she had returned late from her first date.

Time moved.

Other images came and went. She ignored the details, merely watching. Some painful, not so pretty; ugly. The pleasant ones flying past. All of them. Her life.

At 3:40, she snapped alert, wide awake, aware. There it was! *She knew.* The gentle smiling face of Chief Smalls. That was it! Something he had said, had told her dad. If that was true, then perhaps, she could win, but did she have time?

She tore out of the house, her determination renewed, her desire to live strengthened, and her chance to kill Puff reinforced. If only she was right. She prayed.

Dashing over to Sixth Street, her heart raced, her lungs aflame like molten brass. On Davidson Street, she saw the townhouses, but which one? Crossing her fingers, she bounded onto the front porch of the third apartment and banged loudly on the door.

"Open up, please," she screamed. "I know you're in there. If you can hear me, let me in."

No response.

Banging louder, she yelled. "You've got to let me in," she pleaded. "I can save you from the cat. Please."

The curtain peeled back. "Who are you? What do you want?"

"Open up. Let me in so---."

"No!" The figure in the window started to move away.

"Please don't go. Don't go!"

"What do you want?" the voice crackled.

"Do you have a son?" Brittany held her breath; expectant.

"No."

"A nephew?"

"No, and go away. Please."

Brittany thought fast. "Does a little boy with a yellow cat live somewhere in this unit?"

"Next door. Now leave us alone."

Brittany ran next door. She started to knock, but afraid they might not answer, she took her coat off and draped it over her head. This was not the time to take any chances. She didn't. She crashed through the window, lunging head first through the glass, landing into the living room. Dazed, she stumbled, regained her footing, and then darted upstairs where she found the mother and son huddled together in the bedroom. Both shook with terror.

Out of breath, she gripped the boy's shoulder. "It's alright," she muttered. She stared hard into the boy's terror-stricken eyes. "You had a little, yellow cat, didn't you?" Please say something. Our lives depends on it."

"Yes," the boy said timidly.

"She died, right?"

Again. "Yes."

"How," Brittany asked firmly, "did your cat die?"

The boy started to cry.

"Don't cry, please." Brittany gripped the boy's shoulders tightly. "You have got to help me, Roscoe. How did your cat die?"

The boy stopped sobbing. "My name is not Roscoe."

"Oh, but you are," Brittany snapped. "Now, how did your cat die?"

The little, white boy sighed. "I was digging up some flowers in the garden, down by the parking lot---."

"And?"

"Some funny-looking water started coming up out of the ground."

"Please." Brittany begged, "what happened?"

"My cat drank some of the water. She died."

"Oh, my God!" Brittany exhorted. "Thank you." She ran to the bedroom window. "Show me."

The buy pointed. "Down there."

"Please, Jesus, let me have time." She turned towards the boy. "Your shovel. Where is it?"

"There."

"It is going to be just fine," Brittany assured the mother, "but pray all the same." Then she dashed out of the room and down the steps, into the kitchen. She snatched a glass from off the table before bounding out of the door.

A crack of lightning split the sky.

Thunder rumbled.

Big gobs of rain splat themselves upon the bare earth.

And Brittany ran fast.

When she reached the garden, she grew dizzy. This was the spot where the creek had been. "Oh my God!" she groaned. She stabbed the shovel into the damp ground, the thrust making only a brown dent in the hard dirt. She thrust again. Then again. More times. And finally, the earth broke. She scooped up a tiny mound of the moist dirt and kicked the blade of the shovel into the scarred recess once again. *Pay-Dirt!* She quickly removed the chunks of earth and flung them out of her way.

It rained.

Once more the shovel went down and once more topsoil was removed. Frantic, Brittany fell to her hands and knees, pulling at the ground with her fingers until she had excavated a small stick, then a few round stones. Digging deeper, she bore into the earth, removing a clump of petrified debris that revealed an oval, gashing hole. She clawed at the hole, extending her fingers into the darkness, then wetness.

The rain suddenly stopped and the sun burst through and Brittany quickly filled the glass with water from the creek.

Running home, tired and soaked, she rushed into the kitchen. "Please, God, please," she prayed. "Let's this work."

She grabbed two cans of cat food from the pantry and dumped the tuna fish into a bowl, pouring in the dirty water, thoroughly mixing the contents. She stirred. She prayed. She looked at the time.

6 minutes left.

It wasn't wise to think because she was frightened. Plus, time was running out too fast, so she quietly withdrew inside herself and did exactly as Roscoe had instructed her to do if she ever needed to summon Puff. She mentally screamed.

"PUFF!"

A few long seconds elapsed. Nothing. The young girl became extremely nervous, wondering if her relationship with Puff was strong enough to lure her away from the furious blood-letting she, no doubt, was engaged in. Brittany wondered if she possessed the general powers of the mind to make the cat come. More seconds faded. And then more. Still yet more. Then.

"Meow."

4.5 minutes.

Fresh blood covered the cat, offering a brilliant contrast to her normal yellow coloring, and Brittany counted under her breath as Puff's harsh demeanor gradually changed, going soft......softer. The fur was in retreat, becoming less active, less extreme.

4 minutes. And counting.

Time was dissolving. It promised little, but it urged her to action. It was NOW or NEVER! Almost at once, she plopped the bowl on the floor, then looked away, her breathing almost nonexistent. Puff circled the bowl. More determined, Brittany pushed the bowl with her foot to within an inch of the cat's nose. She waited. She watched. And she went limp as Puff licked a small chunk of the food and chewed it. The yellow cat's tongue flicked out for more and more.....and more.

Brittany exploded into hot, boiling tears. Joy. Relief. But above the sound of her weeping and the cat's greedy slurping, came the noise and din of aircraft. She gazed out the window and helicopters filled the air.

"Oh my God!" She glared at the ticker tape, streaming across the bottom of the TV screen like a banner.

2.5 minutes.

And Puff was still alive.

She snatched up the phone from its cradle on the wall. She dialed a number. *"Die!"* she mouthed silently at Puff while she prayed her call would be answered.

"Hello."

"The Mayor, please."

"I am the Mayor." The voice was tense, tight, tired.

"Call them off."

"Who?"

"The bombers."

I'm sorry, but I can't. May God have mercy upon------."

"Tell them we need more time," Brittaney yelled.

"I am so sorry."

"We need more time," Brittany pleaded. "You don't understand."

"There is no more time. I'm sorry." The Mayor sighed in defeat. "We were a wonderful city, but we lost."

"No, we didn't, Mr. Mayor. Puff just died!

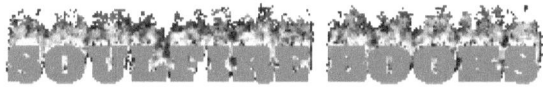

"Is this some kind of joke? I----"

"It's no joke, Perkins. Call it OFF.

"On what proof," Perkins demanded, "the desperate plea of some hick-town Mayor?"

"Dammit, Perkins, there is no time to split hairs. Abort the damned mission at once."

"We finally have White House approval-------."

"Abort the fucking mission, Perkins. Now!"

Shortly thereafter, the rankled voice of the General crackled in the cockpit of the bombing sortie, and one-by-one, the planes did an about-face in the clear, southern sky and headed back to base in tight formation.

FINAL CHAPTER

Within minutes, the entire nation was totally gripped by the mesmerizing news footage of the young, blonde girl, emerging slowly from the townhouse in Charlotte, carrying the motionless, blood=splattered body of the yellow cat. The world breathed a collective sigh of gratitude.

With measured, careful footsteps, the girl looked straight ahead, walking regally, her face caked with mud and tears. Television cameras zoomed in, picking up and falling into the rhythmic cadence of her walk. At the courthouse, the Mayor and his entourage waited to accept the dead cat.

He seemed so far way, Brittany noted, as her legs went up and down in very slow motion towards the Mayor. She wanted her footsteps to hurry up, to move fast, GO. She wanted to get on with her life, to get rid of Puff. She looked down at the silver serving platter and grimaced in disgust at Puff's still, lifeless body, but she also experienced a wild elation. If only her parents were alive. Chief Smalls also.

She took one more step. The Mayor was growing bigger.

Another step.

She had done it! She had been right, but what if her lucky hunch had not paid off. She grew faint. Charlotte would be dead now. Thank God, she had remembered Chief Smalls saying that the white people who had moved into First Ward somehow took on the spirit and character of the black folk who had lived there before they had been displaced. If that was so, she had guessed that there had to have been a white kid with a yellow cat, the spiritual counterparts of Roscoe and Puff. And she had been right. She smiled. She was going to be a great lawyer, after all.

Hot emotions flooded her young, body, overwhelming her so she ran the rest of the way to where the Mayor waited. Suddenly, she wanted to finish it, to get it over with. To get her brother and to get back home.

Reaching the Mayor, she handed him the dead, yellow cat. She uttered one word.

"Puff!"

MEET GIBRAN TARIQ, AUTHOR & CEO OF SOULFIRE BOOKS

For most of my life, I was the guy most wannabee thugs wished they could be. Officially declared a "menace to society", I was sentenced to 30 years in federal prison for my role as mastermind of a series of daring bank robberies in the 70s. Two involved shootouts. One with the police. The other with a citizen in a bank parking lot where I narrowly missed being killed. While confined, I took part in an even more daring prison escape.

As a boy, I toyed with the alphabets like most kids my age played with marbles, and from the start, there appeared to be a household conspiracy to convert me into a writer. By the time I was ten, I possessed a private library fit for a scholar, a new typewriter, a big desk, and plenty of blank paper. By 11, I had mastered the dictionary, was a whiz at Scrabble, and was an honor roll student in school. At twelve, I had completed my first novel.

By my 13th birthday, I had discovered hustling and adopted "the streets" as my home. By 14, I was in reform school for assaulting a police officer.

While at Stonewall Jackson Training School, I was the first black deemed smart enough to work in the Print Shop where I became a prized reporter for the institutional newspaper. I served a year and a day, and with hardly any delays, I embarked on a personal crime spree.

At fifteen, I was tried as an adult and sentenced to prison although I was still a juvenile. At Polk Youth Center, I was the youngest convict there, but I rapidly evolved into Public Enemy Number One. I held the record for going to the "Hole" for rule violations such as fighting, extortion, and my all-time favorite, starting a riot.

While in the Youth Center, I acquired my high school diploma at 16, wrote my first play, turned militant, and when released at 19, went to New York to join the Black Panthers, but discovered heroin instead. Both the revolution and writing would have to wait as a drug habit left little room for anything else.

After serving ten years in the feds(1973-1983) for multiple bank robberies, I was framed by state authorities and I served another ten years(1983-1993) for a robbery I **DID NOT** commit. Then I served another ten years in the feds (1997-2007) for being the alleged "king-pin" of a notorious heroin distribution ring.

In prison, I turned back to what I had turned my back on: writing. I wrote every day for 10 years and I was even placed in "the hole" for publishing my first book. The administration in the Atlanta pen said that publishing a book was tantamount to "running a business while confined". I fought the case and after thirty days was let out of segregation, but this is what earned federal prisoners the right to publish a book without fear of reprisal.

Now, as CEO and Founder of SoulFire Books, I want to help break your "literary" chains. Free Yourself. Visit us at www.soulfirebooks.com

Media Contact; www.soulfirebooks09@gmail.com
980 299 0867